I0740962

TABLE OF CONTENTS

Love Creek Productions
Sponsor of the
Annual Off-Off-Broadway Original Short Play Festival

Production Director: Sharon Fallon
Stage Manager: Paige M. Van Den Bury
Stage Manager: Ron Hirt
Lights: Whitney Chaiet Bessegato

OFF-OFF BROADWAY FESTIVAL PLAYS
TWENTY-FOURTH SERIES

The Last Cigarette
Steven Fechter

Flight of Fancy
Louis Felder

Physical Therapy
Jean Reynolds

Nothing in the World Like It
Frances Galton

The Price You Pay
Arlene Hutton

Pearls
Nira Lipner

Ophelia
Karen Sanford

A Significant Betrayal
Le Wilhelm

A SAMUEL FRENCH ACTING EDITION

SAMUELFRENCH.COM
SAMUELFRENCH-LONDON.CO.UK

ISBN 978-0-573-62717-0

www.SamuelFrench.com
www.SamuelFrench-London.co.uk

THE LAST CIGARETTE

by

Steven Fechter

For Holly

THE LAST CIGARETTE
by
Steven Fechter

with

ANGELA . . . . Serena Berné

HOWARD . . . . Brian John Driscoll

Directed by Larry Geddes

Originally produced by
The Tuesday Group

ABOUT THE AUTHOR

Productions include *Schiele* (Ohio Theatre), a multimedia work on the life of the artist Egon Schiele, *The Land-Surveyor* (Westbeth Theatre) an adaptation of Kafka's *The Castle, Intimacies* (Ensemble Studio Theatre), and *Newspaper Play* (HERE). Steven is a member of The Dramatists Guild.

CHARACTERS

    ANGELA: early 30s
    HOWARD: late 30s

SETTING

    Place: A bar in Santa Monica, California
    Time: Present

(A smoky bar. Center stage is a small table with two chairs on either side. On the stage left side of the table sits ANGELA, sipping on a martini and smoking a cigarette. She is about 33, dark hair, pale skin, very striking. She wears a shimmering green strapless dress. A string of pearls adorn her neck. In the background the music of cool jazz is heard. ANGELA takes a drag from her cigarette and stares dreamily into the smoke. HOWARD enters from upstage left, drink in hand – it's scotch on the rocks, a double. He stops, stares at ANGELA, slugs back some scotch, then sits at her table. He's about 38, wears dark slacks, dark polo shirt, and light tan sports coat. HOWARD smiles at ANGELA. She nods, not as an invitation, but to simply acknowledge that, for the moment, he has not violated her space.)

HOWARD. There was once this proud, beautiful woman. We were together. Then we weren't together. After the breakup, I called her every year on her birthday. On the night of her birthday I did the following: I put on my silk bathrobe, poured myself a glass of fine burgundy, an eighty-nine if I could find it, and settled into my leather club chair. I waited until just before midnight, passing the time rereading my favorite sonnets of Shakespeare. "My mistress' eyes are nothing like the sun ... Love is my sin, and thy dear virtue hate ... Be wise as thou art cruel." Then I dialed her number. *(He sips on his scotch. She sips on her martini.)* When she picked up the phone and said –
ANGELA. Hello?
HOWARD. – I would say nothing. Not even breathe – so I could hear her breathe. I waited. Again, this time a little impatiently, she repeated –
ANGELA. Hello!
HOWARD. Then quietly I hung up. *(Pause)* Want to know why I hung up?
ANGELA. *(She takes a drag on her cig, looks at him.)* Sure.
HOWARD. Because I simply needed to hear her voice. *(Pause)* You want to know why I needed to hear her voice?
ANGELA. Sure.
HOWARD. To know that she was alive. So that I could live another day, another month, another year.

(He looks off.)

ANGELA. How long did you do this?
HOWARD. Seven years. Then I stopped.
ANGELA. Why'd you stop?

HOWARD. Because I finally realized how fucking stupid it was.

ANGELA. Thank you for sharing that very poignant story with me. Now I think you should go.

(HOWARD watches ANGELA take a drag from her cigarette.)

HOWARD. You take great pleasure in smoking.

ANGELA. Do I?

HOWARD. You should see yourself. It's something out of the past. Some lost image of sophistication, elegance, allure that no longer exists, maybe never existed – except in our imagination of what should have existed. *(She looks at him but doesn't respond.)* Tell me something I didn't know before I met you, and then I'll go.

ANGELA. *(Takes a long, slow drag from her cigarette.)* They're going to close this place tonight.

HOWARD. Who?

ANGELA. The police.

HOWARD. How do you know that?

ANGELA. I got a tip from the bartender. They're going to – what's the phrase? – bust the joint.

HOWARD. Why?

ANGELA. In case you haven't heard, smoking in bars is now against the law.

HOWARD. I knew that.

ANGELA. When I finish this pack, I'm quitting.

HOWARD. You can still smoke at home or in your car.

ANGELA. If I can't smoke in a bar over a dry martini, what's the point? I figured about one third of my adult waking hours have been spent in smoky bars drinking dry martinis. If they're not going to let me do that anymore, I won't smoke.

HOWARD. A woman with principles.

ANGELA. No. A woman with a sense of style. *(She looks at her glass.)* I may give up drinking too.

HOWARD. Let's not get extreme.

ANGELA. If I can't have a cigarette with my drink, what's the point of drinking? *(She turns and looks upstage left.)* Look at them all, lined four deep along the bar. The loyal patrons. The way they're lighting up and sucking it in, you'd think there was no tomorrow. Well ... maybe there isn't. *(Pause)* This was the last smoking bar in Santa Monica.

HOWARD. I heard there's still a few in Burbank.

ANGELA. I heard that too, but who wants to go to Burbank?

HOWARD. Yeah, fucking Burbank.

(He laughs.)

ANGELA. *(Expressionless)* Well, it's been a pleasure.

HOWARD. May I watch you finish that cigarette?

ANGELA. What for?

HOWARD. To give our brief interlude closure.

ANGELA. *(Shrugs)* Sure. *(Pushes pack to him.)* Want one?

HOWARD. No thanks. I don't smoke. *(She looks at him.)* But I appreciate the style.

ANGELA. You might appreciate the style, but you'll never understand it unless you smoke.

HOWARD. Maybe.

ANGELA. It's like that movie, "In a Lonely Place." You know it?

HOWARD. No.

ANGELA. Too bad. Humphrey Bogart, Gloria Graham, who was a tough little bombshell, and directed by Nicholas Ray.

HOWARD. I'll rent it.

ANGELA. Right. *(Takes a long drag from cigarette.)* For me, the key scene is Bogey driving like a maniac until he takes Graham to that lonely place in the road. Remember?

HOWARD. I didn't see ...

ANGELA. I mean, he almost gets them killed when he runs into that other car. Then he nearly beats the driver to death for just mouthing off. And after all that, he turns to Graham and says —

HOWARD. *(In Humphrey Bogart voice.)* I'll take that cigarette now.

ANGELA. Just like that, in that Bogey way —

HOWARD. *(Bogey)* I'll take that cigarette now.

ANGELA. — as if nothing had happened. She's scared of him. Real scared. She still loves him, but she no longer trusts him. When she gives him a cigarette, you're hoping she'll smoke one too. But she doesn't, even when Bogey offers her one. You can tell a lot about a relationship by the way two people smoke together. Anyway, she won't smoke with Bogey. That's when you know it's over, really over between them. *(Puts out her cigarette.)* Speaking of over. I finished my cigarette.

HOWARD. What's the rush?

ANGELA. No rush.

HOWARD. I know you're alone.

ANGELA. I *was* alone.

HOWARD. I mean you're not waiting for anyone.

ANGELA. How do you know?

HOWARD. I watched you from the bar for an hour. Not once did you look around the room. You were with yourself. I liked that. You didn't *need* anyone else.

ANGELA. I don't. I am alone. And I'm glad. I didn't think I would be. *(Pause)* My husband and I just separated after ten years.

HOWARD. How could he let you go?

ANGELA. *(Pause)* When I was a little kid I used to catch butterflies. I would hold them by the wings. *(She snatches something in the air and looks at her fingers as if holding a butterfly. Little girl voice.)* Fly away pretty butterfly. Whatsamatta? Can't fly away? 'Fraid I'll stick ya with a pin? A long, sharp pin? Naaa, I wouldn't do that. *(Normal voice.)* After a few minutes of this childish "fun" I let them go. I could still feel their wing dust on my pudgy fingers. *(She looks at him.)* It wasn't until much later that I realized how a few minutes in a butterfly's life is like ten years in ours.

HOWARD. You didn't answer my question. *(A police siren is heard. ANGELA stiffens.)* What's wrong. The cops? *(The police siren passes.)* False alarm.

ANGELA. I'm not quite ready to quit. *(Looks at HOWARD.)* Want to know the best thing about living alone?

HOWARD. Sure.

ANGELA. I can fart anytime I want. That's freedom. And you know what? I like the smell of my own fart.

HOWARD. Can I ask you something?

ANGELA. Sure.

HOWARD. Would you fart now?

ANGELA. You want me to fart.

HOWARD. If you can. Just a small one. I'd like to smell it.

ANGELA. I think it's time for you to go.

HOWARD. Right after this cigarette. *(He takes a cigarette from ANGELA's pack and offers it to her. She takes it, he lights it.)* I was supposed to meet my friend here. He's getting married. We were going to celebrate. He likes going to dives like this.

ANGELA. Back in the fifties stars like Burt Lancaster and Ava Gardner would go drinking here.

HOWARD. Okay, the dive has history. That's why we decided to come here. My friend's betrothed is a young lady from a well-connected family in Boston. Very old money. He loves her, but the trimmings don't hurt. Anyway, he hasn't shown up. I'm waiting, drinking doubles at the bar, checking out the cheesy old photos on the wall. Then I see *you.* This woman in a shimmering green dress sitting all alone. My God. Green. My mother's favorite color. I remember a green cocktail dress she wore on special occasions. It was a clinging, low-backed number that flared out into a fishtail just below the knees. Maybe they called them fishtail cocktail dresses. I don't know. But it was a hot-looking dress. The kind Marilyn Monroe or Kim Novak would wear to drive Jimmy Stewart crazy.

ANGELA. Vertigo.

HOWARD. Huh?

ANGELA. Kim Novak and Jimmy Stewart were in Vertigo. Alfred Hitchcock?

HOWARD. Oh yeah. Good flick.

ANGELA. Kim Novak never wore a green cocktail dress in Vertigo — with or without a fishtail.

HOWARD. The point is that thirty-five years later, I still remember my mother's dress. I'm three, maybe four, in my pj's, looking out the window as a big black sedan pulls up the driveway. The high school baby-sitter is gazing stupidly at the TV. She can't wait for my mother to leave so her horny boyfriend can drop in and feel her up. My mother comes down the stairs in her green dress and stiletto heels. I can hear the fishtail rub along the banister. It sounds like leaves burning. Then my mother walks out the screen door, arm in arm with a man I don't know. An oily-looking shark with an Adolphe Menjou mustache. He's a complete stranger. But so is she. A glamourous-looking babe I don't recognize.

ANGELA. *(Cutsey)* How's my little monkeyface?

HOWARD. *(Shakes his head.)* She called me monkeyface.

ANGELA. Now you be gooood. You be *very* good while Mommy's gone. Okay monkeyface?

HOWARD. Good, she tells me. This whore is telling *me* to be good. I'm four years old, for chrissakes! What can I possibly do that's bad?

(He laughs.)

ANGELA. Excuse me.

HOWARD. Yes?

ANGELA. Would you mind going away.

HOWARD. You think I have a mother fixation.

ANGELA. *(Sarcastic)* Why would I think that?

HOWARD. The fact is, I never liked my mother, though she was a very beautiful woman. But completely fucked up. And about as maternal as a bat out of hell.

ANGELA. Poor monkeyface.

HOWARD. *(Sharply)* Don't call me that!

ANGELA. Sorry.

HOWARD. *(He looks at her.)* An attractive woman in a green evening dress is one of life's visual pleasures. It's like an orchid in the middle of a desert.

ANGELA. *(Shakes her head.)* Boy, I've heard a lot of come-on lines.

HOWARD. That is not a come-on line.

ANGELA. Sure sounds like one.

HOWARD. I happen to have a first-rate come-on line. Positively irresistible. Absolutely foolproof.

ANGELA. Oh yeah?

HOWARD. But I've never used it.

ANGELA. So tell me.

HOWARD. Maybe later.

ANGELA. Why not now?

HOWARD. I'd rather win you without it. *(She says nothing.)* Why'd you wear it? The green dress.

ANGELA. I need a reason?

HOWARD. A woman like you doesn't wear a dress like that in a dive like this without a reason, even if Burt Lancaster and Ava Gardner got smashed, passed out, and threw up on this very table forty years ago.

ANGELA. First, Burt Lancaster and Ava Gardner would never get that smashed. Second, they had style. True style. Third, you weren't there. Fourth, you weren't even born.

HOWARD. That's true.

ANGELA. And stop calling this place a dive.

HOWARD. It was meant with affection.

ANGELA. I don't care.

HOWARD. Consider it stopped.

ANGELA. Thank you. *(Pause)* I do have a reason for wearing this dress. *(She gets up and slowly walks downstage, holding herself in a regal way.)* I feel beautiful when I wear it. Tonight I wanted to feel beautiful. I saw it in a smart little shop on Melrose Avenue. When I tried the dress on, it was clear. This dress was designed for me. It made me feel like a butterfly that just broke out of its cocoon. I didn't ask the saleswoman how much it cost. I knew I couldn't afford it. So I stole it. *(Pause)* I didn't plan to steal it. I was returning it to the rack when this flashy Mexican doll swoops in clutching the tiniest mini-skirt I ever saw. The whole time she's shrieking.

HOWARD. *(Mexican doll.)* Bruto! Bastardo! Asesinato!

ANGELA. While everyone's trying to calm down this tequila cocktail, I walk out with the dress.

HOWARD. *(Mexican doll.)* Monstroso!

ANGELA. I ran to my car, hit the gas, got on Interstate Fifteen, just so I could drive ninety miles an hour in the desert. I was over the Soda Mountains, halfway to Vegas, before I turned around. What a rush! *(She returns to table.)* Now get me another martini.

HOWARD. How do you like it?

ANGELA. I like it fine.

HOWARD. I meant –

ANGELA. I know what you meant. Just tell the bartender it's for me. He knows how I like it.

HOWARD. I'll be right back.

(He exits stage left.)

ANGELA. It's always the same walk, the same talk, the same look, the same clothes. Dear diary, today I met a nice boy. But where are the men? That's the sixty-four dollar. Bogey, Duke, Gable, Coop. And McQueen. Ahh, McQueen, he was the last one. Not men but ... gods. Warriors with wounds. But now. It's just mortals with money and nice cars ... Midgets. I live with midgets. This is the land of Oz, Toto. This is almost ... unbearable. *(The sound of a police siren.)* Please, not yet. *(The sound passes.)* Thank God. *(She looks at table and touches its surface.)* Even if Burt Lancaster and Ava Gardner did throw up, they would have done it with style.

(HOWARD returns with martini and a double scotch.)

HOWARD. Your martini, madam. Miss me?

ANGELA. No.

HOWARD. I could tell. Watching you as I waited for the drinks. You never looked back. As if you completely forgot about me. I suddenly felt very lonely.

ANGELA. What do you expect?

HOWARD. What I expect?

ANGELA. *(Drily)* After you *win* me.

HOWARD. Nothing less than that my life will change dramatically. Just talking to you has changed me. I feel inspired. Like anything is possible.

ANGELA. *(She nods, sips on her martini.)* If this were a movie, I would turn to the camera and tell the movie audience that nothing is going to happen. *(ANGELA picks up her drink and sits on the edge of table. She crosses her legs and looks at audience.)* That man on screen and the character I play are not going to make love; we are not going to kiss; we are not going to dance; we are not going to fight; we are not going to threaten, blackmail, or throw drinks at each other. We will do none of those things, ladies and gentlemen, because *nothing* is going to happen. So go. Leave by the nearest marked exits. And take your popcorn with you. *(Turns to HOWARD.)* That's what I would do.

HOWARD. You can't do that in a movie.

ANGELA. It's my movie. I can do whatever I want.

(She returns to her chair.)

HOWARD. *(Sips on his scotch.)* If this were a movie, and you said all that, the audience would definitely stay.

ANGELA. No way.

HOWARD. You've just created dramatic tension. Now they'll want to find out if you're right. *Will* nothing happen?

ANGELA. Hey, what do you do?

HOWARD. Do?

ANGELA. Besides annoying women in green dresses.

HOWARD. I live. I eat well enough. I often sleep badly.

ANGELA. I mean for a living.

HOWARD. I work hard at something I enjoy.

ANGELA. You work in motion pictures?

HOWARD. Don't insult me.

ANGELA. I once appeared in a motion picture. I had to lie in a pool of make-believe blood wearing a little white nightie. We did it in three takes. It was a wonderful experience. But I no longer do motion pictures.

HOWARD. Why not?

ANGELA. I got married.

HOWARD. *(Looks at her.)* Motion pictures. Quaint.

ANGELA. So what are you?

HOWARD. Are you trying to label me? I don't like labels. Labels are dangerous. *(He picks up her pack of cigarettes and reads.)* "Warning: Smoking causes heart disease." *(Looks at her.)* Being a man is label enough.

ANGELA. *(Looks at him.)* Warning: Men cause heart disease.

HOWARD. Touché. *(Pause)* You know, I recently attended a party of people who work in "motion pictures."

ANGELA. Is this a story? This sounds like a story.

HOWARD. It's very short.

ANGELA. I've almost finished my cigarette.

HOWARD. I'll be quick.

ANGELA. I just want to be left alone. Okay? Your attention is flattering, but this brief interlude is over. I think we came to closure.

HOWARD. Let me tell this pithy anecdote and then I'll go.

ANGELA. When?

HOWARD. Immediately. As in cut to man exiting bar; cut to woman in bar sitting alone; cut to man in car beating steering wheel with his fists; cut to woman —

ANGELA. Cut!

HOWARD. Right. So I was at this party, and at the center of this throng of second-rate actors, producers, screenwriters, and directors was an actress who was once first-rate. I mean she was first-rate playing loopy heroines in offbeat, low-budget comedies. But after a string of disastrous roles playing ridiculous femme fatales in awful big-budget thrillers, she was now considered second-rate.

ANGELA. Excuse me, but this does not sound like a pithy anecdote.

HOWARD. That was the prologue. The rest is Hemingway.

ANGELA. *(Curt)* Go on.

HOWARD. During a lull in the conversation, this former first-rate now second-rate actress asked my friend what *she* did. I knew that this seemingly benign question invited disaster. But my friend, being a sincere and honest person, answered truthfully.

ANGELA. *(Extremely earnest.)* I work in human resources for a pharmaceutical company. I've been there five years. We just merged with another pharmaceutical company, which now makes us the seventh largest pharmaceutical company in the country. But we're basically the same company, same name, just bigger. We do good work there ... It's really the people ... from the top down. The people are just nice ... and working of course ... with the people ...

HOWARD. As you can imagine, there followed a hideously long pause. Then the conversation turned to some hack director's latest flick. Something called "Frag," about the fragmentation of the consumer society. But with a lot of action, guns, and sex. Anyway, during that pause my friend died.

ANGELA. *(Starts)* Died. She really died?

HOWARD. Actually she was murdered. The actress and the other guests destroyed her with cold efficiency. They deemed her existence insignificant. She was reduced to a nonentity in their presence. *(He leans toward her.)* My friend is a sensitive woman who embraces life as a spiritual journey. A person who, in her free time, works with ceramics and practices Chinese massage. But in that room she no longer existed because second-rate talents with second-rate minds and second-rate souls labeled her "uninteresting." *(He sips his scotch.)* End of story. Should I go?

ANGELA. Yes.

HOWARD. You're making a mistake.

ANGELA. I don't think so. *(Pause. HOWARD doesn't move.)* This friend. Do you love her?

HOWARD. I love her ... like a friend.

ANGELA. Jesus, you gotta be a writer.

HOWARD. If I was a writer, I'd be home writing instead of being here talking to you.

ANGELA. Don't try to throw me off.

HOWARD. Would you see me any different if I was a writer? If you were to describe me to a friend, the first thing you would say is, "He's a writer." Then she would tell you what *she* thinks of writers. Then you'd say, "Come to think of it, he's just like that."

ANGELA. You're not a writer.

HOWARD. Suppose I was an arms negotiator. You know who coined the phrase "weapons of mass destruction"? They've never given me full credit.

ANGELA. Stop!

HOWARD. Would you like to dance?

ANGELA. No!

HOWARD. I could be insane.

ANGELA. You could be. You probably are. But that isn't a profession.

HOWARD. For some people it is.

ANGELA. You're joking with me. You're amusing yourself at my expense.

HOWARD. I never joke. And I wish I could be amusing, but I'm completely humorless. Ask any of my friends.

ANGELA. Now you are joking.

HOWARD. I was insane once. Nothing dangerous. It was benign insanity. It started when my mother hung herself in the garage. I found her hanging from a beam. Bathrobe wide open ... face as purple as an iris. I was thirteen. *(He stands and looks up.)* Mom, what's for dinner? *(He looks down.)* No answer. *(Looks up.)* Mom, can we have pizza tonight? *(Looks down.)* No answer. *(Looks up.)* Mom, Chuck's coming over to help me with my homework. Can he stay over for dinner? Can he? Huh, Mom? Mom? Mom? *(Pause)* No answer. I kept babbling like that until the police arrived.

(He sits down.) A few years later I tried it myself. Same beam, same rope, even the same bathrobe. But the rope was rotted.

ANGELA. Was it green?

HOWARD. The rope?

ANGELA. The bathrobe.

HOWARD. I ... don't remember.

ANGELA. You don't need to talk about this.

HOWARD. *(Voice rises.)* I *do* need to talk about this! All right?

ANGELA. Sure. Whatever.

HOWARD. I went through years of therapy. The usual mix — a little bit of Freud, a little bit of Jung, a little bit of Reich, and some gestalt. *(He stands and starts dancing a samba downstage.)* A little bit of Freud, a little bit of Jung, a little bit of Reich, and some gestalt. I just needed someone who would listen. Then I joined a men's group. That was better. Listening to all those lumpish, hairy bodies with fragile souls was so healing. I hugged more men in two years than all the women I'll ever hug in my entire life. One time I got carried away ... *(He dances stage left than stage right.)* It was during one of our male-bonding things out in the woods. This guy and I are hugging and grunting. The sun is setting. The drums are beating. We're hugging and grunting. The sun sinks deeper. The drums beat faster. Hugging and grunting. Deeper and deeper. Faster and faster. Hugging and grunting. Then kaa-rroooshhh! The horizon explodes into a monster Monet painting. This guy and I stop hugging. The drums stop beating. The sky is blazing. We look at each other and say, "Fuck it." *(He stops dancing.)* Neither of us had ever had sex with a man before. Afterwards, when we joined the others, I felt fine and rather pleased with myself. But my partner confessed our transgression to the leaders. We were promptly kicked out of the group.

ANGELA. That wasn't nice of them.

HOWARD. *(Returns to his chair.)* I didn't mind. I broke a rule. I'm okay now.

ANGELA. Okay with what?

HOWARD. With myself. With women. With the world. I know what I want. Most people don't know what they want.

ANGELA. What do you want?

HOWARD. A long-lasting relationship. A home. Children. I'm looking for the real thing. "Lifestyle" is not in my vocabulary. "Laid back" are two four-letter words. When I saw you I saw something I wanted.

ANGELA. I can't help you.

HOWARD. I don't want you to help me. I want to help you.

ANGELA. You can't help me.

HOWARD. Tell me what you want.

ANGELA. Another martini.

HOWARD. Is that all?

ANGELA. Right now it's the only thing I need. I'm sorry, but I don't want you. I don't want anything like you. We are two very different people, coming from two very different worlds. Understand?

HOWARD. *(Pause)* I hear you.

ANGELA. I'm sorry.

HOWARD. I'm going to get your martini, and then I'll go.

(HOWARD exits stage left. ANGELA rises and walks downstage, holding out her arms.)

ANGELA. Thank you, ladies and gentlemen, for that warm welcome. You make me feel like a queen. Me. A poor little girl from Santa Ana. But I have nothing but fond memories of that dreary hick town. How can I ever forget those tough Mexican boys in junior high who taught me Spanish? And I was a quick learner. Amor, ahora nos vamos a la casa. *(Smiles)* As you know, I recently spent some time in the hospital. But they say everything is going to be okay. I'm all right now. *(Stares angrily at audience.)* I said I'm all right! *(Smiles)* Thank you, thank you very much. A million kisses for everyone who sent me cards and letters. Wow. It was overwhelming. There was one postcard I'll never forget. A beautiful message from twelve-year-old Christopher Hodges, who said he was praying for me every night. God bless you, Chris. *(She cups her hand over her eyes.)* I see a lot of friends sitting out there. I missed you. I love you. And speaking of love, I'm going to sing a song that I always sing about this time. It was written by a very good friend of mine, Mr. Cole Porter. *(Waves)* Hi, Cole. Yeah, it's about love. And heartache. It's about laughing when we're with that special someone, and it's about crying when we're all alone. So alone we want to die ... to disappear forever into the darkness. But then, somehow, we always find the light to live another day. You know what song I'm talking about. And if you feel like it, sing along, but softly. Okay? *(She looks stage right.)* Harry, give me a little intro.

(With intensity, she hums a few bars of "Night and Day" then returns to table. HOWARD enters with her drink.)

HOWARD. Miss me?

ANGELA. No. Watching me?

HOWARD. Yes.

ANGELA. What did you see?

HOWARD. I saw a woman sitting quietly at her table, so still she could have been a model in a life-drawing class.

ANGELA. Aren't those models usually naked?

HOWARD. You asked me what I *saw*.

ANGELA. *(Laughs)* That's funny.

HOWARD. I'm not funny. Trust me. *(ANGELA stops laughing.)* What's the matter?

ANGELA. I never trust a man who says "trust me."
HOWARD. Why?
ANGELA. A trustworthy man wouldn't need to say it.
HOWARD. Then I will never say it again.
ANGELA. *(Looks at him.)* Nothing is going to happen.
HOWARD. I have a house on the beach. Come with me. There's a full moon. Have you ever seen a full moon on the beach?
ANGELA. *That's* your come-on line?
HOWARD. *If* I tell you my come-on line, you'll know it.
ANGELA. And if every guy who told me he had a house on the beach had a house on the beach, there wouldn't be any more beach.
HOWARD. You don't believe me?
ANGELA. There isn't a full moon.
HOWARD. Three-quarters.
ANGELA. Half.
HOWARD. Two-thirds.
ANGELA. Half.
HOWARD. Poetic license. *(She takes out another cigarette. He lights it for her.)* I'd like to walk down the Promenade at Pallisades Beach holding your hand. *(Pause)* Want to know why?
ANGELA. Sure.

(They stand.)

HOWARD. So people can see the luckiest man in L.A.

(They walk around the stage, staying well apart.)

ANGELA. *(Looks at him.)* Why don't you hold my hand now?

(They stop.)

HOWARD. *(Surprised)* Right now?
ANGELA. Here's my hand. Hold it. Hold it as if we were walking down the Promenade on Pallisades Beach this very second. *(He walks toward her to take her hand.)* But after you hold it, you must promise to leave. *(She offers her hand. HOWARD stops.)* Don't you want to hold it?
HOWARD. You come across as being a cool woman.
ANGELA. Do I?
HOWARD. But I think that inside you there is great heat.
ANGELA. *(Amused)* Heat.
HOWARD. Inside, you are a churning volcano, a steaming geyser, a passion flower about to burst, a voodoo dance to feverish desires.
ANGELA. *(She holds herself with her hands.)* Is that what you think?
HOWARD. Yes.

ANGELA. Too bad. You'll never know.
HOWARD. I *will* hold your hand.
ANGELA. Good.

(She offers her hand.)

HOWARD. But I have a proposal. If your hand feels cooler than mine, I'll walk out of this bar and you'll never see me again; however, if your hand feels warmer than mine, I can stay with you all night.

(He holds out his hand. Pause. She pulls her hand away.)

ANGELA. Let's not hold hands.
HOWARD. Whatever you say.

(An awkward pause. They return to table.)

ANGELA. Tell me what your can't-miss come-on line is.
HOWARD. And waste my strongest card? I'm not a fool.
ANGELA. What have you got to lose?
HOWARD. What have I got to gain?
ANGELA. Tell me your come-on line, and if it's as good as you claim, if it knocks my socks off ... I'll dance with you. But if it lays in a bucket like wet cement, you will exit without a word. Agreed?
HOWARD. I like a challenge. *(He sips his scotch, then looks at her.)* My come-on line is very brief. It consists of two words: I'm dying.

(Long pause.)

ANGELA. Shall we?

(HOWARD and ANGELA dance. The music swells. They hardly move, clutching each other like people afraid of drowning. Music dies. They sit down.)

HOWARD. Something has happened.
ANGELA. We only danced.
HOWARD. You only danced. *(Pause)* And your hands are warmer than mine.
ANGELA. *(Pause)* How long?
HOWARD. To live?
ANGELA. If it's not too ...
HOWARD. I don't mind. Forty more years – if I don't get hit by a minivan.
ANGELA. *(She stares at him.)* Forty *more* years?

HOWARD. That's right.
ANGELA. *(She throws her martini in his face.)* You dirty sonofabitch!
HOWARD. Why did you do that?
ANGELA. *(She throws her martini in his face.)* You dirty sonofabitch!
HOWARD. Why did you do that?
ANGELA. *(She throws her martini in his face.)* You dirty sonofabitch!
HOWARD. Why did you do that?
ANGELA. That was a horrible thing to do!
HOWARD. Calm down.
ANGELA. You tricked me!
HOWARD. I didn't say it was true.
ANGELA. You took advantage of my emotions.

(She covers her face.)

HOWARD. Hey. Don't cry. I *told* you it was a come-on line. *(Pause)* You must think I'm quite an asshole. Listen, hey, listen to me. I don't do this sort of thing. Approach strange women? Try to sweep them off their feet with sweet declarations of love? Boldly charm their hearts with my audacious bravura? Roll them over with balls of brass? Are you serious? That is not me. I mean, this is so out of character. *(Three-year-old voice.)* I like you. Wanna play fishy-fish? First we'll play little fishy-fish and ... and then we'll play BIG fishy-fish. Okay? *(Normal voice.)* Listen to me! Will you please stop crying?

(ANGELA uncovers her face. She's laughing.)

ANGELA. I'm not crying.
HOWARD. What the hell's so funny?
ANGELA. It's not important.
HOWARD. You puzzle me ... you mystify me.
ANGELA. Why did you say you were dying?
HOWARD. I only meant that living without you is *like* dying.
ANGELA. A metaphor.
HOWARD. Metaphors can also be true.
ANGELA. *(She reaches for her cigarette pack.)* I'm going to have my last cigarette and then you're going to leave.
HOWARD. I'll go.
ANGELA. Good.
HOWARD. I can see it's hopeless.
ANGELA. That's right.
HOWARD. Before I go –
ANGELA. No.
HOWARD. Dance with me one more time.
ANGELA. No!

HOWARD. Let that moment be my last memory of us.

ANGELA. The cops are going to bust in any minute. *(She looks out over audience.)* The last smoking bar in Santa Monica. Tomorrow it will be just like the others. Cleaner, fresher, but no style.

HOWARD. All the more reason to have this last dance. To celebrate style. To mourn its passing. To remember the way it used to be, in all its hard-edged, ironic glory.

ANGELA. *(Shakes her head.)* Don't.

HOWARD. Please. Do me this last kindness. And then I'll disappear — like a dream. By tomorrow morning you won't remember my face.

(HOWARD stands up and extends his hand. Pause. ANGELA takes his hand. They dance. The music swells. They hardly move, clutching each other like people afraid of drowning. Then they kiss. It should be nothing more or less than the first kiss of two people strongly attracted to each other. The music dies. They break and sit down.)

ANGELA. Good bye.

HOWARD. Good bye? You said nothing would happen. But we danced. You threw your drink in my face. I made you laugh. And now you let me kiss you.

ANGELA. I never stopped you.

HOWARD. What?

ANGELA. I never stopped you from kissing me.

(He leans over and kisses her.)

HOWARD. And now we've kissed again. Next thing you know, we'll be making love.

(He starts to kiss her again, but she pulls away.)

ANGELA. You haven't yet asked what I do?

HOWARD. You were once in a motion picture in which you immortalized a death scene that rivals Juliet's. You drink martinis and smoke cigarettes in stylish bars haunted by the ghosts of Hollywood idols. You wear bewitching green dresses when you want to cast spells on lonely men.

ANGELA. Before you leave, I promise to tell you what I do.

HOWARD. I'm not leaving.

ANGELA. I *will* tell you.

HOWARD. If it makes you happy.

ANGELA. It doesn't make me happy.

HOWARD. I want to know how you learned to sit like a queen. I want to know how you attained the language of fallen angels. I want to know why it took me so long to meet you when I've known you all my life. I want to know how any man could let you go. *(She giggles.)* My God. You're giggling.

ANGELA. Sorry.

HOWARD. No. It's wonderful.

ANGELA. It's just that ...

HOWARD. What?

ANGELA. I was waiting to see ...

HOWARD. Yes?

ANGELA. Whether you noticed.

HOWARD. Noticed what? *(Smiles)* You farted. *(She nods.)* I love it.

ANGELA. Bullshit.

HOWARD. In a way.

ANGELA. Too strong?

HOWARD. No, not at all.

ANGELA. You're not just saying that?

HOWARD. *(Inhales)* It's got some bite, I'll admit. But it's earthy, robust, round, full-bodied. *(Inhales)* I detect tobacco, spice, coffee, and chocolate. It's got backbone. Character. Nothing worse than an insipid fart that can't get past your nostrils. Yours goes right into my head, my lungs. It fills me. It is a fart as true and real as the stars and moon.

ANGELA. No one has ever spoken to me like that before.

HOWARD. Then you've been listening to the wrong people. Shall we go?

ANGELA. Wait. I haven't smoked my last cigarette.

HOWARD. Smoke it later.

ANGELA. No. It's got to be here. *(She takes the cigarette out of the pack, fingers it, but doesn't put it in her mouth.)* You know, it's funny that you said you were dying.

HOWARD. It wasn't meant to be funny.

ANGELA. But it was.

(Pause)

HOWARD. Why is that funny?

ANGELA. Because I *am* dying.

HOWARD. *(Pause)* That's a metaphor.

ANGELA. No.

HOWARD. We're all dying ... by degrees.

ANGELA. Yes. But my dying is – how shall I say – more accelerated.

HOWARD. *(He stares at her.)* How accelerated?

ANGELA. The story you told about calling that woman every year on her birthday. *(Pause)* That could never happen to me because ... I probably won't be around on my next birthday.

HOWARD. *(As if he didn't hear her.)* You want to know the real reason I stopped calling her?

ANGELA. It's not important.

HOWARD. *(Bangs table with his fist.)* I *have* to tell you! *(Pause)* The last time I called her ... I go through the ritual ... you know ... the robe, the burgundy, the leather club chair. Five minutes to midnight, I call her. I settle back. I sip my burgundy. I hear her say –

ANGELA. Hello?

HOWARD. I listen to her breathe. Then she says –

ANGELA. Victor, I know it's you. Stop fucking calling me on my birthday!

HOWARD. Now you know why I stopped?

ANGELA. Because she destroyed the little dreamworld that you so carefully constructed when she called out your name.

HOWARD. *(Pause)* My name isn't Victor.

ANGELA. Oh.

HOWARD. What killed me was that for seven years she thought that sick little puppy who called her was Victor – whoever *he* was – the little prick!

ANGELA. What is your name?

HOWARD. Howard.

ANGELA. Howard. My name is Angela.

HOWARD. *(Smiles)* Angela. In the city of angels.

ANGELA. What do you do?

HOWARD. I'm an investor.

ANGELA. You mean you invest money?

HOWARD. Mostly I invest other people's money. So they can make more money. Of course I do all right myself. The economy's booming, Angela. It's a good time to invest.

ANGELA. Howard.

HOWARD. You don't want to be left behind when everyone's cashing in. Of course you need to know where the good investments are. Know their potential for growth. What are the risks? The benefits? You make projections. You look into the future ... you have to sense –

ANGELA. Howard, look at me. *(HOWARD looks at her.)* I'm a dying person.

HOWARD. No.

ANGELA. Yes. That's what I am. Dying is what I do. I'm dying of breast cancer, Howard.

HOWARD. You can't die, Angela.

ANGELA. The doctors want to operate. They want to cut them both off. Do the radiation thing. Do the chemo thing. But I won't let them. I won't let them fuck around with my body. Not *my* body. I'm going to die in style. If you live in style, you die in style.

HOWARD. You can't die, Angela.

ANGELA. Even if I did everything they said, my chances are only fair. That was the word the doctor used, "fair." He said if I did nothing it would kill me in a year. But if I did everything they advised, I had a *fair* chance of living three to five more years. I thanked him and walked out. I haven't been back since. *(She tries to light her cigarette, but her hand trembles. HOWARD lights it for her.)* You really have a house on the beach?

HOWARD. Yes. *(Pause)* You know ...

ANGELA. Don't say it. Don't tell me how medicine is making tremendous advances all the time. Don't. I've got six months. A year, maybe. I'm looking for someone – man, woman, or dog – to love me until I die. I may ask that person to help kill me. I'm looking for a very, very special love. *(She looks at him.)* Do you have what it takes, Howard?

(He slowly looks at her.)

HOWARD. Yes. *(He kisses her.)* You're worth it.
ANGELA. I'm worth what?
HOWARD. Every day, every hour, every minute, every second.
ANGELA. And?
HOWARD. *(Struggling)* And ... I ...
ANGELA. I will love you until your dying breath.
HOWARD. Goes without saying.
ANGELA. I want you to say it.
HOWARD. They're words, Angela.
ANGELA. Say it, Howard.
HOWARD. I will love you until your dying breath.
ANGELA. Good.

(She smokes. HOWARD watches her.)

HOWARD. Another martini?
ANGELA. Sure.
HOWARD. Be right back.

(He gets up and starts to exit stage right.)

ANGELA. Where are you going? The bar's over there.
HOWARD. I have to go out and make a phone call.
ANGELA. Call here.
HOWARD. *(Pause)* It's out of service.
ANGELA. Let me come with you.
HOWARD. I'm just going to call my friend. The one who I was supposed to meet. See if he's okay. I won't be a second. Then I'll get you a martini.
ANGELA. I don't want you to go.
HOWARD. *(Laughs)* Go? I'm not going. I'm coming right back.

(She goes to him.)

ANGELA. Don't leave me! I can't bear it!

HOWARD. Angela.

ANGELA. *(She clutches his arm.)* I'm scared. I don't want to die alone. There's no one out there. Understand? I'm alone. I need you to be with me. That's all. Just be with me. You don't even have to love me. Just *be* with me. Please.

HOWARD. *(Calmly.)* I love you. I'll never leave you. I'm coming right back. And then we'll be together. Trust me.

ANGELA. *(She looks at him and lets him go.)* Sure.

(She clutches his arm.)

HOWARD. I love you. I'll never leave you. I'm coming right back. And then we'll be together. Trust me.

ANGELA. *(She looks at him and lets him go.)* Sure.

(She clutches his arm.)

HOWARD. I love you. I'll never leave you. I'm coming right back. And then we'll be together. Trust me.

ANGELA. *(She looks at him and lets him go.)* Sure.

(He exits stage right. She returns to the table. There should follow one to two minutes of real time. ANGELA knows that HOWARD is not coming back, and though the temptation is great, she never looks around the room. Instead, with great effort and terrible strain, she quietly smokes the rest of her cigarette. Then she puts it out and stares dreamily into the wafting smoke.)

ANGELA. Nothing ... is going to happen.

(Lights fade to the sound of a police siren. The siren gets progressively louder until it is almost deafening. Blackout.)

COSTUME PLOT

ANGELA:

    Evening dress -
       shimmering green, strapless
    Pearl necklace & earrings
    Black evening pumps
    Elegant small purse

HOWARD:

    Light tan sports coat
    Dark polo shirt
    Dark slacks
    Casual loafers (no socks)
    Expensive-looking watch

PROPERTY LIST

ON STAGE:

    1 small round table
    2 "cafe" chairs
    1 ashtray
    1 pack of cigarettes
    1 cigarette lighter
    1 martini glass - half full

OFF STAGE:

    2 martini glasses -
       full with olives
    3 tumbler glasses -
       scotch on the rocks

SET DRAWING

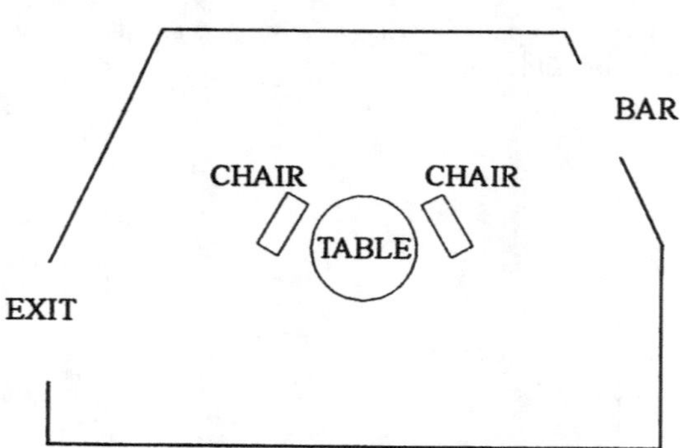

FLIGHT OF FANCY

by

Louis Felder

To Stace, Nick, Linda

FLIGHT OF FANCY
by
Louis Felder

with

JOE . . . . Lou Felder

TRACEY . . . . Cynthia Forbes

Directed by Louis Felder

Produced by
Actors Alley of North Hollywood, California

ABOUT THE AUTHOR

FLIGHT OF FANCY is part of *Going Places* – a collection of Louis Felder's one-acts: (produced at the Interact Theatre Company and at Theatre East in Los Angeles), which includes *Sparks, The Magic Kingdom,* (winner of the National Pathways Drama Competition), *Trumps, Lemonade on the Promenade, Jungle Express,* and *The Man in the Red Suit.* Other plays include *Far From The Tree, Tribune, Taking Issue, People's Choice, Cold Feet,* and *Hot Set.* His novel, *Rocky Libido in San Francisco* is published by Contact Editions. He is a member of the Dramatist Guild and the Golden West Playwrights.

CHARACTERS

JOE: About 55, an experienced salesman on the road.
TRACEY: About 25, a pretty Marketing MBA from Stanford, on her first business trip.

SETTING

Place: Portland Oregon Airport, Cocktail Lounge.
Time: The present, about 6 PM.

(On stage is a counter in the airport bar, facing the "window" where people stand, drink, and watch the planes. We hear flight announcements and the whine of jet engines.)
(A man, JOE, about 55, enters from the bar area carrying a drink, a garment bag, a salesman's case, and a bag of cornchips – a feat he performs with the nonchalance of experience.)
(He is sipping his drink as a woman, TRACEY, about 25, staggers in with a suitcase, an immense garment bag, an attache case and a shoulder purse. She is pretty, wearing a suit and skirt, and manages to carry her drink.)
(She dumps her entire load near his feet at the counter and stands next to him. They stare straight ahead as if looking through the window. She ignores him, preferring to be left alone.)

JOE. Arriving?
TRACEY. Departing.
JOE. Why didn't you check those?
TRACEY. *(Testy)* I imagine I will ... when I'm ready.
JOE. You can't board with that stuff, not the suitcase anyway.
TRACEY. *(Irritated)* I thought I'd have a drink first. Okay?
JOE. *(Under his breath as he turns away.)* Somebody had a tough day.
TRACEY. Sorry. Tough week.
JOE. Yeah, Portland can be a tough town ... Where'd you stay – the Hilton?
TRACEY. Sheraton.
JOE. I'll tell you, next time try the Cascade Motor Lodge. *(Pointing out the name on a book of matches, which she ignores.)* The Cascade Motor Lodge. It's right downtown, good coffee shop, real nice people, and you can't beat the price nowheres. *(She doesn't respond.)* Now, over in Spokane, there's a real bargain – the Thunderbird Motel. You want to know why? *(She doesn't respond.)* I'll tell you why.
TRACEY. You must be in sales.
JOE. *(Nodding)* You?
TRACEY. Marketing.
JOE. Same thing.
TRACEY. Not really.
JOE. What are you, one of them M.B.A.'s or something?
TRACEY. That's right.
JOE. Everybody on the road is in sales except them. They're in "marketing." ... Who do you work for?
TRACEY. Allied Paper. Royal Container Division.

JOE. Oh yeah? That's a big outfit. What do you sell?

TRACEY. Fiber packaging.

JOE. *(Snide)* Cardboard boxes.

TRACEY. What do *you* sell?

JOE. *(Handing her a card.)* Refrigerated cases, for supermarkets.

TRACEY. *(Reading)* "Paramount Showcase and Fixture. Joe Waggoner, rep."

JOE. I cover six Western states.

TRACEY. *(Sighing)* And how was *your* week, Joe?

JOE. Just two days – down in Salem. Re-doing a Pick and Shop. Wrote up two Super-Igloos, an Eski-mobile unit, and a Frigid-Queen.

TRACEY. Heading home?

JOE. To Boulder ... eventually. After Denver, Grand Junction, Durango, Pueblo, Fort Collins and Greeley.

TRACEY. Long trip.

JOE. About ten days more.

TRACEY. I guess you're anxious to get home. *(She gets no response.)* I bet you miss your wife and family. *(She gets no response.)* Right?

JOE. So where are you from, er – ?

TRACEY. Tracey.

JOE. Tracy, California?

TRACEY. Tracey Baker.

JOE. Oh, Tracey's your name. I thought it was the town where you're from – Tracy, California.

TRACEY. No.

JOE. I used to sell in Tracy, – good territory, Northern California. So where are you from, Tracey, where do you live?

TRACEY. San Francisco – but I'm not sure where – where I'll be living ... or moving, or going to – now ... I don't know.

JOE. Getting married? Transferred?

(JOE waits but gets no response. Finally she drinks and slams down her glass.)

TRACEY. Do you know Eckart and Miller in Beaverton? Turpentine, lacquer, furniture polish?

JOE. Heard of 'em.

TRACEY. Do you know Mister Eckert?

JOE. No. You call on him? How was he? Tough? Huh? Tough sell?

TRACEY. In the past, he's always bought four-gallon divider cartons, for wholesale, that's all, but now he's going retail, *shelf-retail!* – with twenty-four ounce squeeze bottles shipped by *box-dozen.*

JOE. Jackpot. You nail him?

TRACEY. Maybe. It's kind of up in the air.

JOE. You didn't sign him?

TRACEY. Not yet.

JOE. If you couldn't close him in a week, Tracey, I think you lost him.
TRACEY. He's always bought from us.
JOE. But you didn't get the new order.
TRACEY. No.
JOE. Just the re-order.
TRACEY. No.
JOE. What'd you come up with? *(Near tears, TRACEY can't talk; she shakes her head.)* Blank? You come up empty? What did they say at the home office?
TRACEY. Haven't told them yet.
JOE. You got anything to balance out? How's the rest of the trip?
TRACEY. This was my only call. And my first call!
JOE. Of the month?
TRACEY. Of my career! My first and only call for Allied! And I lost the account!
JOE. Oh man. *(JOE thinks, snaps his fingers, and the old-pro salesman springs into action.)* Okay, phone him back, this guy Eckert, call him back, cut the price, two for one, rebates, give him a color TV under the table, anything, keep him talking.
TRACEY. I can't.
JOE. Find another angle. Come on!
TRACEY. He said to call him back if I changed my mind.
JOE. *(With smug canniness.)* Okay, yeah, about what? The price? Sure.
TRACEY. About going out with him.
JOE. Good! Take him to a ball game, buy him a beer —
TRACEY. *HE'S A PIG!*
JOE. So what? Listen, Tracey, in selling — marketing, you sell a product, sure, but you also sell yourself.
TRACEY. Sell myself?
JOE. Yeah, so buy him lunch, tell a few jokes, have a few drinks, —
TRACEY. I took him to lunch. He wanted something else under the table.
JOE. Kickback?
TRACEY. That's where his hands were.
JOE. You mean — he wanted ...
TRACEY. *SEX!*
JOE. Yeah, well, there's that kind of problem, sure. I never had it myself. Well, once. This manager of a Value King in Coeur d'Alene — I sold him a Polarama Two Thousand — top of the line, so I bought him a big lobster dinner. And walking back in the parking lot, he put his hand in my pocket. Surprised the hell out of me.
TRACEY. What did you do?
JOE. I took it out. Told him he better take a cab. Next day he canceled the order.

TRACEY. They didn't cover this at Stanford. Sex as a marketing tool.

JOE. I got to be frank, looking at you, I can see you're gonna have that problem maybe a lot, 'cause most women in sales – in your marketing, I see 'em around wearing these blue raincoats like they're in the Air Force. But you, Tracey, you're just too darn pretty.

TRACEY. And that's a drawback?

JOE. It don't have to be. Hell, make it an asset. Use it.

TRACEY. I should meet him at the Sheraton?

JOE. *(Realizing)* Oh, so the door's still open. Oh, that's why you didn't check your luggage. You can maybe still get the order if you ...

TRACEY. I haven't decided anything yet – about what I might do. Or not do.

JOE. *(Consulting his note book.)* Listen. if he wants a woman, there's a number here in Portland you can call, right downtown, real nice people, they set up the whole thing, put it on your Visa Card, American Express –

TRACEY. He wants *me!*

JOE. Well, you're not thinking of – no, you're not that type. Are you? No.

TRACEY. *(Uncertain)* No.

JOE. No! Then tell him to go to hell!

TRACEY. And there goes my career.

JOE. No way, your first call. So maybe you lost a customer –

TRACEY. And that goes on my record. Back at headquarters – my district manager – he'll write up my performance evaluation – I won't be sent out again, Joe. I'll be dead in the water.

JOE. There's other companies.

TRACEY. *(Shouting)* I don't want other companies! I want Allied! That's the company I targeted! They're expanding, across the Pacific. That was my major at Stanford, my thesis – "Packaging Opportunities, Pacific Rim." I begged to be sent out; they gave me a set-up, an old client, I did the research. What could go wrong? Everything!

JOE. Well, those are the breaks; you can't sweat it.

TRACEY. Oh? How would *you* feel if you went home with a minus?

JOE. It's happened.

TRACEY. What did you tell *your* boss?

JOE. I told him the units was priced too high, no one could figure the specs, and he was the one screwing up not me!

TRACEY. *(Impressed)* Really?

JOE. He didn't buy it. He sent me on the road ... for three weeks ... in Montana ... in January, Jesus. Ice on the road, supermarkets half buried in snow, and I'm selling refrigeration equipment. Nothing.

TRACEY. And what did you tell your wife when she said: "Welcome home, darling, how was your trip?"

JOE. She never asked that. "Welcome home, darling." She never said that ... Never ... Don't matter.

TRACEY. You have children? I'll bet *they're* happy to see you.

JOE. My daughter is; she's sixteen. My son, though, – he just hangs out with his buddies in them off-trail pick-ups, you know, the trucks with the big wheels. Drives all over Colorado, Utah, Idaho. I don't know.

TRACEY. How old is he?

JOE. *(Ashamed)* Thirty.

TRACEY. What does your wife do?

JOE. Oh, she – she stays at home – takes care of my son's baby – man, cries like a siren. But she always watches her show, you know that network home shopping on TV – she buys all that stuff, figurines, gold chains, – we got tea cozies, and toilet seat cozies, you know them shag carpets you put on the toilet so the lid falls down when you're taking a leak, you know? No. Hell, we got 'em in different colors for every season of the year.

TRACEY. She doesn't go out?

JOE. To the Post Office. That's about it.

TRACEY. But when you get home – I'll bet she wants to make up for lost time, go out to dinner, dancing.

JOE. No, she – no, she don't – we eat at home ... My daughter's a good cook though, a real good cook. In fact, when she gets out of high school, you know what she wants to be? A travel agent. She wanted to be a model – she's got a real pretty face, but she likes her own cooking too much ... Makes her unhappy ... Me too.

P.A. ANNOUNCEMENT. Continental Airlines, Flight Number 415 to Denver, now boarding at Gate 7.

JOE. That's mine. What's your flight?

TRACEY. United 370 to San Francisco.

JOE. Are you going to take it? ... Or meet that guy at the Sheraton?

TRACEY. If I had a choice, Joe, I'd just as soon stay right here talking to you.

JOE. Me too. I don't look forward to these trips no more. Or even heading home.

TRACEY. I'm not looking forward to anything.

JOE. If I had a choice, I'd rather be flying off to ... some place else.

TRACEY. Oh, so would I. Anywhere. Anywhere.

(TRACEY tries to hold back her tears but she can't. She closes her eyes and begins to cry. JOE puts his hand on her back; without realizing it, she lets her head fall against his chest and cries. JOE, not knowing what to do, puts his arm around her.)

JOE. Oh, gee.

(As JOE comforts her in silence, they become aware of an announcement.)

P.A. ANNOUNCEMENT. Passengers with Tropical Magic Tours may now board at Gate Twelve for service to Honolulu, Figi, Samoa, Tonga, Papeete, Bora Bora, Pago Pago, Singapore and Macao.

(As JOE and TRACEY listen to the announcement, they look off. Every romantic port of call conjures up a dream, of escape, of blue lagoons and swaying palms. Still in each others' arms, they seem to gaze across the Pacific. Then they look at each other. They seem about to kiss. But it can't happen. JOE takes his arm away. He finishes his drink.)

TRACEY. Thanks for talking to me, Joe.

JOE. What I told you about selling – selling yourself – that don't mean you got to ... aw, don't listen to me. I never had a career, I only got a job. You do whatever you got to do; I won't throw no rocks at you.

(JOE picks up his garment bag and starts to leave.)

TRACEY. Joe? I hope we run into each other again. Maybe in the Denver Airport. I'll tell you what: I'll say: "Welcome home, Joe. How was your trip?"

(JOE is touched, emotionally moved. He tries to be casual and think of something to say.)

JOE. Good luck with your – your Pacific Rim. That's a big territory. You ought to do okay.

(He wants to say something more but can't think of any words and steps away. She sips her drink. JOE looks back, reaches out as if longing to embrace her, but bows his head and simply pushes his bag of cornchips towards her and leaves.)

P.A. ANNOUNCEMENT. United Airlines, Flight Number 370 to San Francisco, now boarding, Gate 47.

(TRACEY stares straight ahead and sips the rest of her drink. Lights fade and out.)

THE END

COSTUME PLOT

TRACEY:
Business suit with mid-thigh skirt, fashionable.

JOE:
Old sports jacket, ugly tie, mailman shoes.

PROPERTY PLOT

Counter

Tracey:
attache case
shoulder purse
suitcase with wheels
garment bag
drink

Joe:
salesman's case
garment bag
drink
bag of cornchips
address book
matches
business card

SOUND EFFECTS

Airport sounds
Jet engines
Three flight announcements

GROUND PLAN

A counter, center, down stage.

PHYSICAL THERAPY

by

Jean Reynolds

For Nancy, Dawn and JoAnn
and for
The Abingdon Theatre Company

PHYSICAL THERAPY
by
Jean Reynolds

with

SADIE . . . . Dawn Gowins

BEULAH . . . . JoAnn Mariano

Directed by Nancy Rogers

Presented by
Abingdon Theatre Company

PHYSICAL THERAPY was originally produced under the title THE GOOD FIGHT by Expanded Arts, New York City, Jennifer Spahr, Executive Director with the same director and cast as above.

ABOUT THE AUTHOR

JEAN REYNOLDS' plays have been produced Off and Off-Off Broadway and regionally. She has received awards from the Kennedy Center Fund for New American Plays, Beverly Hills Theatre Guild – Julie Harris Playwriting Competition, and Playwrights First.

CHARACTERS

BEULAH: a woman who wouldn't tell you her age.
SADIE: Beulah's friend,
               a woman who wouldn't tell you her age, either.

SETTING

Place: Beulah's porch. Beulah and Sadie in rocking chairs.
Time: A summer evening

*(AT RISE: BEULAH's porch. BEULAH and SADIE sit in rocking chairs,
sunk in, as if they've been there a long time. A summer evening. They
are drinking gin.)*

SADIE. Heard you had a man coming around.
BEULAH. That's right.
SADIE. Heard he comes round several times a week.
BEULAH. That's right.
SADIE. What's he coming round for?
BEULAH. *(Pause)* Things.
SADIE. Oh.
BEULAH. You know.
SADIE. Oh.
BEULAH. Things men do.
SADIE. Oh. *(Pause)* What?
BEULAH. He's a professional man.
SADIE. What profession?
BEULAH. The profession of helping those who need help.
SADIE. Now, Beulah, I am not prying –
BEULAH. I know, dear.
SADIE. But I heard talk.
BEULAH. I heard talk too, you know.
SADIE. What?
BEULAH. I heard you're getting an operation.
SADIE. That's right.
BEULAH. It's true, then?
SADIE. That's right. I'm down for the count.
BEULAH. Why didn't you tell me, Sadie?
SADIE. Didn't want trouble.
BEULAH. Trouble?
SADIE. Look here, Beulah, it's a necessary operation and you mustn't
try to talk me out of what's necessary.
BEULAH. Don't go through with it.
SADIE. I'm not going to discuss it.
BEULAH. Why can't we discuss it?
SADIE. Don't want to.
BEULAH. Don't want to?
SADIE. Don't want to.
BEULAH. All right.
SADIE. I will not subject myself to your powers of persuasion.
BEULAH. Friendly advice is what I offer.

SADIE. Can we get back to our original topic?

BEULAH. Which is?

SADIE. The man you have coming round –

BEULAH. Don't want to discuss it. Two can play that game, you know.

SADIE. Fine.

BEULAH. Fine.

SADIE. Must be something off about him.

BEULAH. Off?

SADIE. A bit off. Must be.

BEULAH. Nothing off. He's nice.

SADIE. Nice?

BEULAH. That's right.

SADIE. Nice, is he?

BEULAH. I can't get out like I used to – and oh, I used to. I can't do what I used to do. He comes round to ... to help.

SADIE. Rake the yard, put up the storms, that kind of thing?

BEULAH. No.

SADIE. What's he do?

BEULAH. Who?

SADIE. The man you have coming round.

BEULAH. He was assigned to me.

SADIE. A nurse?

BEULAH. No.

SADIE. What say?

BEULAH. He's no nurse.

SADIE. That's what I thought you said. *(Pause)* What's he do, then?

BEULAH. What's he do? He does ... well, I guess you'd call it physical therapy.

SADIE. Physical therapy?

BEULAH. Yes, physical therapy.

SADIE. You need physical therapy?

BEULAH. Came through a service. One of those ... you know ... one of those services. You know. One of those specialized services. You know.

SADIE. No. I don't know.

BEULAH. Very discreet.

SADIE. Specialized?

BEULAH. Very.

SADIE. Well now, what do they specialize in?

BEULAH. They specialize in what men are good at. You know what men are good at. It's not raking leaves. It's –

BEULAH & SADIE. Physical therapy.

SADIE. Lordy! Lordy!

BEULAH. Want the number?

SADIE. Lordy! Lordy!

BEULAH. Want the number? Call up today ... or tomorrow. Want the number? Come on, I know you want the number.

SADIE. Don't have time for it.

BEULAH. Beats a doctor all to hell.

SADIE. I have a serious medical situation for which I must seek remedy. I am on the ropes.

BEULAH. Physical therapy is the answer.

SADIE. Ah.

BEULAH. Ah? What's ah mean?

SADIE. Nothing.

BEULAH. Must have a meaning.

SADIE. No.

BEULAH. Must have a meaning, your saying, "ah."

SADIE. No.

BEULAH. There was a quality to it.

SADIE. What sort of quality?

BEULAH. A definite sort of quality. An insinuation.

SADIE. Ah.

BEULAH. Stop that!

SADIE. What?

BEULAH. Saying ah.

SADIE. Oh. Didn't realize. "Ah" is an unconscious expression.

BEULAH. Of what?

SADIE. If it's unconscious, I don't know, do I? I believe in the unconscious. Perhaps, as you say, there is a reason I said ah, but I don't know it. Because it's unconscious. *(Pause)* It could be that there is a reason. But I don't know it.

BEULAH. Don't say it again.

SADIE. Okay.

BEULAH. Gets on my nerves.

SADIE. Won't say it again.

BEULAH. Thank you. *(Pause)* How about another drink?

SADIE. All right.

BEULAH. Put in olives. Olives are good in gin. He likes olives.

SADIE. Who?

BEULAH. Frank. That's his name. Frank. He's a knockout.

SADIE. A knockout?

BEULAH. That's right.

SADIE. You called up and they sent him over?

BEULAH. Easy as pie.

SADIE. It's dangerous, you know. Calling up a service ... a service of that type. It's dangerous, you know.

BEULAH. I'll tell you what's dangerous.

SADIE. What?

BEULAH. What you signed up for. That's what's dangerous. Very dangerous, actually. I wouldn't recommend it.

SADIE. No?

BEULAH. Having been through it myself. I wouldn't recommend it. Nasty business, that. No, I would not recommend it. Of course it's up to you. Naturally. But, no, I would not recommend it. So many things can go wrong. Leave you in a bad way. Worse off, you know. It can kill you.

SADIE. Kill me?

BEULAH. Sorry to be so blunt.

SADIE. It can kill me?

BEULAH. It can.

SADIE. I wasn't told that. Nobody told me that.

BEULAH. Well, they wouldn't, would they? They're after the almighty buck. What's it to them if they lose you along the way? They still get their almighty buck.

SADIE. I don't think they'll kill me.

BEULAH. Want another olive in your gin?

SADIE. No, I don't think they'll kill me.

BEULAH. I've got a supply of olives. Sent over from Italy.

SADIE. Do you think they'll kill me?

BEULAH. Once a month.

SADIE. Once a month?

BEULAH. Once a month olives arrive.

SADIE. Olives?

BEULAH. Got a standing order actually.

SADIE. They won't kill me.

BEULAH. A standing order.

SADIE. They won't.

BEULAH. Frank and I eat a lot of olives. A standing order, you see.

SADIE. It could happen.

BEULAH. Direct from Italy.

SADIE. You hear about things like that.

BEULAH. They make mistakes.

SADIE. Mistakes?

BEULAH. Sometimes they do. They make mistakes.

SADIE. It could happen, but it's very slim.

BEULAH. Once they sent stuffed mushrooms.

SADIE. Almost impossible.

BEULAH. It was a mixup.

SADIE. Mixup? Beulah, this man you have coming round? How nice is he?

BEULAH. Very nice. *(Pause)* The point is ... The point is, you don't have to do it.

SADIE. Do what?

BEULAH. What you signed up for.

SADIE. I'm scheduled.

BEULAH. You don't have to ... to do what they say. I did what they said and they almost killed me.

SADIE. It's their job. They're trained.

BEULAH. They're trained to worship the almighty buck. That's what they're trained to do. Drink all right, is it?

SADIE. Eh?

BEULAH. Your drink?

SADIE. It's fine. It's ... all right. *(Pause)* Where's Frank now?

BEULAH. It's Tuesday. He visits his mother on Tuesday.

SADIE. Oh. *(Pause)* What if they kill me?

BEULAH. Can happen.

SADIE. Might not.

BEULAH. Might not.

SADIE. Didn't happen to you.

BEULAH. A miracle. A miracle it didn't happen to me.

SADIE. But I'm scheduled.

BEULAH. Cancel.

SADIE. I'll think it over.

BEULAH. Cancel.

SADIE. I'll postpone.

BEULAH. Cancel!

SADIE. Cancel?

BEULAH. Fight them. Like Jack Dempsey. Remember Jack Dempsey?

SADIE. Yep.

BEULAH. Frank and I enjoyed the stuffed mushrooms.

SADIE. The what?

BEULAH. The stuffed mushrooms.

SADIE. Oh.

BEULAH. Jack Dempsey was a fighter. He wouldn't let them get him. Sugar Ray Robinson.

SADIE. He was good.

BEULAH. Rocky Marciano was good.

SADIE. They were fighters, that's right.

BEULAH. But in modern times ... the best fighter was Joe Louis. Remember him?

SADIE. Joe Louis. He was the best. That's right.

BEULAH. That's modern times.

SADIE. Max Schmelling.

BEULAH. Schmelling? Well ... he got ... he got killed.

SADIE. He got killed. Yes, he did.

BEULAH. It was awful.

SADIE. Awful.

BEULAH. If you ... if you ...

SADIE. If I got killed?

BEULAH. If you did —

SADIE. This is just why I didn't want to discuss it. You put the terror of death in me. You make my knees knock together and my teeth jump up and down. Now stop it, Beulah.

BEULAH. But what would I do if –

SADIE. If I got killed?

BEULAH. I couldn't go on.

SADIE. You'd go on. Because that's what people do. People go on.

BEULAH. No one to have gin with. No one to talk to.

SADIE. What about Frank?

BEULAH. That's physical therapy.

SADIE. I'd like to get me some of that physical therapy.

BEULAH. It ain't bad, but it ain't talk.

SADIE. I haven't had physical therapy in a long time.

BEULAH. I'm not trying to cause trouble, but if anything happens to you –

SADIE. Stop! Stop it now! I must have this operation! Do you understand! I must have it! I must! I must!

BEULAH. *(Pause)* I'm sorry, Sadie.

SADIE. I know.

BEULAH. I'm sorry.

SADIE. I'll be all right.

BEULAH. You will?

SADIE. I'm Joe Louis.

BEULAH. Joe Louis, he's the best.

SADIE. The best.

BEULAH. A fighter.

SADIE. A fighter.

BEULAH. Tell you what.

SADIE. What?

BEULAH. I'll come with you.

SADIE. You will?

BEULAH. I'll keep watch. I'll keep my eyes on them. If anything goes wrong, the smallest thing, anything at all, I'll ... I'll ...

SADIE. You are a formidable woman.

BEULAH. I'll bring my boxing gloves.

SADIE. A lovely gesture. Lovely. I appreciate it. Puts my mind at ease. Puts my mind at ease, knowing you'll be in my corner.

BEULAH. I may even wear boxing trunks.

SADIE. Heh, heh. *(They drink their gin. SADIE eats an olive.)* These are good olives.

BEULAH. Very good.

SADIE. The man ... the man who comes around ...

BEULAH & SADIE. Frank.

SADIE. He's a knockout, you say?

BEULAH. Keeps my pulse up.

SADIE. What's the number?

END OF PLAY

COSTUME PLOT

BEULAH:
Red floral print dress

SADIE:
Blue floral print dress

PROPERTY LIST

Gin bottle
Ice bucket
Ice tongs
Plate of pitted olives

SET DRAWING

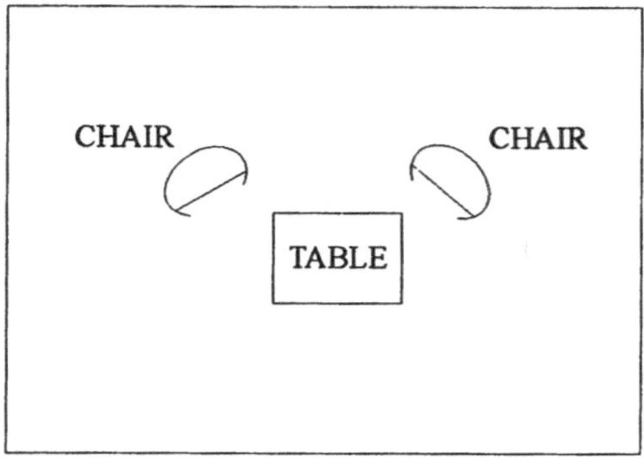

NOTHING IN THE WORLD LIKE IT

by

Frances Galton

This play is dedicated to John Edmunds,
Alice E. Garcia, Shelley Ray, and Alice Gold
(the original cast members), who devoted their
unpaid time and professionalism to bringing
my words to life.

NOTHING IN THE WORLD LIKE IT
by
Frances Galton

with

CLARISSA . . . . Alice Gold

EDIE . . . . Shelley Ray

DOUG . . . . John Edmunds

Directed by Frances Galton

Nothing in the World Like It was originally produced jointly by American Playwrights Theatre, Inc., and Caicedo Productions as part of an evening of one-acts entitled *At Work and Play: Five Short Plays Celebrating Women's History Month* at the John Houseman Studio Theatre Too, New York City with the following cast:

CLARISSA . . . . Alice E. Garcia

EDIE . . . . Shelley Ray

DOUG . . . . John Edmunds

ABOUT THE AUTHOR

FRANCES GALTON has worked as an actress, director, playwright, producer and teacher. Several of her plays have been produced Off-Off-Broadway, the most recent being *The Boarder, Lucy's Waltz* and *Stragglers* in 1998. She studied at HB Studio, Columbia and CUNY, where she earned a Ph.D. in Drama and taught for 18 years. She is a member of the Dramatists Guild.

CHARACTERS

    CLARISSA: An aging Black woman from the South.
             (This role can be adapted for any Southern woman.)
    EDIE: A college junior.
    DOUG: A college senior.

SETTING

    Place: New York City
    Time: The 1980's

(The cafeteria of a public college in New York City. CLARISSA is arranging food on a counter. EDIE enters, dressed bizarrely, looks around, sees no one, moves to the food counter, and examines the items on it. CLARISSA watches her for a moment.)

CLARISSA. C'n I he'p you, young lady?
EDIE. No, thanks. I don't want anything.
CLARISSA. I don' believe *that*. Eve'yone come in here want *something*.
EDIE. Oh, I want lots of things: good grades, more money ...
CLARISSA. Those we ain't got. But how 'bout some ... cookies?
EDIE. No, thanks. I'm into a new style of eating. No junk food.
CLARISSA. We don't carry no junk food. Eve'ythin's fresh as a daisy ... This here fruit? Sliced it up myself this mornin'. Try some?
EDIE. I'm not into fruit today. I feel like something ... quieter.
CLARISSA. Then how 'bout some nice, quiet ... cottage cheese?
EDIE. Cottage cheese isn't high on my list.
CLARISSA. Ya sure are picky. I 'member you come in here and buy candy all a time.
EDIE. I'm off candy. I saw this program on TV about eating right, and they said candy has no food value.
CLARISSA. Eatin' right's impo'tant. We gotta take care of our selfs, nobody gonna do it for us.
EDIE. I know. The right food gives you a certain buoyancy ... *(Seeing that CLARISSA doesn't understand the word.)* ... A good feeling, like walking on air.
CLARISSA. So long's you don't try walkin' on water. *Nothin'* you eat's gonna do *that* for ya.
EDIE. I'm not looking for miracles. I just want to do what's right: eat right, dress right ...
CLARISSA. You runnin' for pres'dent or somethin'?
EDIE. If you want to be happy, you have to do the right things.
CLARISSA. Well, I hope you *very* happy, whatever you doin'.
EDIE. I'll just have some milk.

(She picks up a small carton of milk and hands CLARISSA some coins.)

CLARISSA. Can' go wrong with milk, it's one thing *do* work miracles. Make your bones strong, your teeth white, put a *natural* color on your cheek 'stead of like a made-up kewpie doll.
EDIE. You think I look like a ... You think I look *weird?*

CLARISSA. No more'n any the other kids come in here.

EDIE. My boyfriend thinks I look weird. He never *said* it, but I can see it in his eyes.

CLARISSA. He mus' like you for what you are, no matter what you look like.

EDIE. Oh, he likes me a lot. It's *me* that's confused about *him*.

CLARISSA. What's confusin' you, darlin'? Tell ol' Clarissa.

EDIE. I'm not sure what I want ... Part of me wants to do one thing, and part of me ... What do you think's more important, going to college or getting married? For a girl my age, I mean?

CLARISSA. If *I* was your age, I'd get myself a education 'fore I got married. If I'd a had a education, I wouldn't a been no counter lady. I'd a been workin' in a office with all them other office girls, sittin' at a big desk with a typed writer and a telyphone all my own ...

EDIE. Is that what you wanted to be, a secretary? Sitting in an office all day?

CLARISSA. Better than standing on your feel all day.

EDIE. Better than raising kids?

CLARISSA. They's not the same thing. Can't do nothin' without a education 'cept clean up after other people ... and I *hates* cleanin' up.

EDIE. No one likes their job nowadays. My mother hates hers, you hate yours ... I'm not going to spend *my* life at a job I hate.

CLARISSA. Can't always do what you like, darlin'. Some things you *gotta* do 'cause they right, like you say ... That answer your question?

EDIE. Sort of ... Thanks for your help.

CLARISSA. Any time.

(CLARISSA begins to cover the food on the counter as EDIE moves to a table, sits and drinks her milk. DOUG enters, an athletic young man in a sweatsuit carrying a jacket and a large canvas bag, which he drops next to EDIE's table as he straddles a chair. He is flushed and in high spirits.)

DOUG. Sorry I'm late. Coach kept us ... Whew! What a workout! I must've used every muscle in my body. Why don't *you* work out?

EDIE. Working out makes me tired ... *You* must be tired.

(CLARISSA exits with the newspaper.)

DOUG. Naw, just thirsty. What're you drinking, milk? I thought you hated milk?

EDIE. Milk's good for you. Gives you strong bones.

DOUG. Still wearing my old jacket? Maybe I'll give you this sweatshirt when the season's over. I won't need it after this year.

EDIE. You make me feel like a ... a rag-picker.

DOUG. These things are expensive. My father worked overtime to buy them.

EDIE. Then let your father wear them.

DOUG. Very funny.

EDIE. You know I hate hand-me-downs.

DOUG. You buy things at thrift shops. Aren't they hand-me-downs?

EDIE. That's different.

DOUG. The only difference is you *pay* for them. I'm *giving* them to ... Forget it, I'll give them to my brother. He'll be glad to get them. Save my old man a bundle ... What else they got to drink here?

EDIE. Soda, juice, I don't know. Go see.

DOUG. *(Approaches the counter and looks over the food items. Calling.)* Anyone here? *(To EDIE.)* Isn't anyone here?

EDIE. She's in back.

DOUG. *(Calling)* Hello? Anyone home?

(CLARISSA enters drying her hands on a paper towel.)

CLARISSA. He'p ya, sir?

DOUG. What took you so long?

CLARISSA. When Nature call, you gotta answer.

DOUG. Yeah, well, Nature's got to wait his turn ... What do you have to drink?

CLARISSA. What you want?

DOUG. If I knew, I wouldn't be asking, would I?

CLARISSA. Coffee, tea, juice, milk ... and soda.

DOUG. Any ice for the soda?

CLARISSA. Ice give ya cramps.

DOUG. I didn't ask what it *gives* you. I asked if you *had* any.

CLARISSA. Ice all gone. We closin' soon.

DOUG. Then give me a Coke. Fast.

CLARISSA. Can on'y go so fast.

(DOUG pays and returns to the table.)

EDIE. *(An awkward silence. Finally ...)* Fall Festival's next week. Are you going?

DOUG. I have basketball practice next week, every day. Coach wants to nominate me for M.V.P.

EDIE. What's that?

DOUG. Most Valuable Player. I'd be up against guys from all over the city. It'd be great if I won. Not for myself, but for my folks ...

(During the following scene, CLARISSA packages and removes food from the counter, exits and returns several times.)

EDIE. And for the school. You'd be a hero, a celebrity. It would be in the papers ...

DOUG. I'd do it for my father, not the school. He'd get the most out of it. Doesn't say much, but he beams when I do something good ... When I made the Dean's List last year? You should have seen him. As if *he* was the one ...

EDIE. Must be proud of you.

DOUG. More than proud. Like he's living his life over again through me, but he expects *me* to be better than *him*. Not that he's a failure or anything. Just that he wants me to *be* somebody, so he can show me off to his friends. It used to bother me, but now I can see his point ... What's the matter, Edie? You ... mad at something?

EDIE. All you do is talk about your father.

DOUG. He's important to me. Anything wrong with that?

EDIE. People don't spend their lives talking about their ...

DOUG. He's my *father*. Just because *your* father took off and you never see him ...

EDIE. That has nothing to do with it.

DOUG. Yes, it has. A boy's father's the most important person in his life. If *you* were a boy ...

EDIE. Well, I'm not. So let's just drop it. Okay?

DOUG. *You* brought it up ... What's bothering you? Something on your mind?

EDIE. What makes you think something's bothering me?

DOUG. You wanted to see me, and now you're acting ... I don't know ...

EDIE. Weird? Why don't you say it?

DOUG. *You* said it, not me ... What did you want to see me about?

EDIE. I just wanted to see you. Haven't seen you in almost a month.

DOUG. I study at night. It's my last year, and I want to keep my grades up.

EDIE. I miss you, you know that? ... It's ... lonely without you ...

DOUG. What about your other friends? Joan and Cathy?

EDIE. Joan has a job after school, and Cathy is going out with Eric.

DOUG. Well, make new friends, or get another job. You're over the flu, you can go back to the supermarket.

EDIE. I hated that job. I worked all day Saturday and spent Saturday nights alone ... How about after the game? I could wait for you ... ?

DOUG. We have a meeting with the coach after every game, and then I ... I go out with the guys ... You don't want to come, Edie. You don't like basketball ...

EDIE. What about Sundays?

DOUG. I gotta rest on Sundays. Coach wants us to be in top form ...

(CLARISSA re-enters, sits at counter and pretends to read the paper.)

EDIE. So you're saying you don't want to see me, is that it?

DOUG. It's not I don't want to see you. I'm just ... I don't have time to fool around any more ... You should join a club or something so you don't hang on to one person all the time.

EDIE. You think we've been fooling around ... ?

DOUG. You know what I mean.

EDIE. I'm busy too. I take care of my brother and sister after school and study on weekends. I don't have a lot of time either ... I'm getting hungry ... I think I'll have a cookie. *(Approaches the counter. To CLARISSA.)* Any cookies left?

CLARISSA. On'y one.

(Hands EDIE a large chocolate chip cookie; EDIE pays and returns to her table.)

EDIE. They say cookies aren't good for you, but when we were small, my mother gave us a cookie every time we cried, and *we're* all healthy today ... Want a piece?

DOUG. No, thanks. I've got to go.

(Starts to get up.)

EDIE. Tell me one thing: are you seeing ... sleeping with ... someone else?

DOUG. Are *you?*

EDIE. No.

DOUG. Neither am I.

EDIE. Is that the God's-honest truth?

DOUG. You want a signed statement?

EDIE. Well, you're not sleeping with me.

DOUG. You can't spend your life in bed. There's a whole world out there ...

EDIE. You said you wanted to get married ... ?

DOUG. Course I want to get married. Some day, when I'm ready.

EDIE. *I'm* ready now.

DOUG. No, you're not. You're too young. We both are.

EDIE. Cathy and Eric are the same age as us, and they're getting married in June, right after graduation. And they've been going together less than a year.

DOUG. Look, Edie, you don't just get married. You need a job, and a place to live, and money in the bank ... You can't just rush into it . What's this sudden urge to get married? Is it because Cathy and Eric are getting married?

(Slight pause.)

EDIE. I'm ... pregnant, Doug.

DOUG. How many months?

EDIE. One or two.

DOUG. Don't you *know?*

EDIE. Two. It was right after Labor Day ...

DOUG. How did *that* happen? I thought you were on the pill?

EDIE. It ... just ... *happened.*

DOUG. You can get an abortion.

EDIE. I can't afford an abortion. It's at least two hundred dollars.

DOUG. I can give you about a hundred. Can't you get the rest somewhere?

EDIE. I don't want an abortion.

DOUG. Why not, for Chrissakes? You're not a Catholic.

EDIE. I ... want to ... to do the right thing.

DOUG. You think it's right to tie us both down with a kid? You think it's right to bring a kid into this world when you can't support it?

EDIE. If you mean, is it right to get married and have this baby, yes, I think it's right – for me, for you ...

DOUG. It's not right for *me.* I'm not ready to be a father yet.

CLARISSA. *(Approaching the table with a large trash bag.)* You through with this soda, sonny?

DOUG. Yes, take it ... And don't call me sonny!

CLARISSA. Sorry, *sir. (Throws can into trash bag.)* We closin' now, folks.

DOUG. *(Ignoring her.)* Edie, listen. *I* want to do the right thing too, but I can't get married now. I owe my folks something. They expect me to be a success, and I can't do that with a baby to support.

EDIE. A baby's beautiful. It's something to hold and love and play with ...

DOUG. You're living in a fantasy world! Wake up, for Chrissakes! A baby ties you down. I'm not ready for that. I've got to make it on my own, show my father I'm his equal ... You'll *have* to get an abortion.

EDIE. I don't want to! I want to live *right,* like other people.

DOUG. If you're so intent on living right, I could tell you a few things you're doing wrong. Such as the way you look. Your hair, and all that crap on your face. You think I could bring you home and say, 'Look, Pop, this is the girl I'm going to marry?' He'd think I was crazy.

EDIE. You're just trying to get out of it! You *have* to marry me, you're the father!

DOUG. I don't *have* to do anything. I've got girls calling me every day. I can pick and choose. I don't even know if I *am* the father, or if you're really pregnant or just giving me some cock-and-bull story ...

EDIE. You're a bastard!

DOUG. I'm going to *make* something of myself, and no weirdo's tying me down with a baby story ... Go find yourself another sucker ...

EDIE. Don't worry, I wouldn't marry you if you begged me ... I'm *not* pregnant, you're right. I was just testing you ...

DOUG. I knew it! Just looking for a meal ticket, like my father warned me ... It's over, Edie. Finished!

EDIE. Good!

DOUG. And don't call me. I've got better things to do.

EDIE. What? Polish your father's shoelaces?

DOUG. Bitch!

(He exits hurriedly.)

EDIE. Wait, Doug ... I'm ... sorry ... *(Seizing her stomach, she doubles over and moans softly.)* Oh-h-h-h-h ...

CLARISSA. *(Rushing to her.)* You all right, miss? You better sit down ... I knowed you was carryin' soon's you come in. They's somethin' 'bout a baby makes a woman look special.

EDIE. I'm not special. I'm not anything.

CLARISSA. You an expectin' mother. That's *very* special.

EDIE. I don't know if I *want* to be a mother.

CLARISSA. It's a hard decision, 'specially when you all by yourself. That boy don't know nothin'. He got a lot to learn.

EDIE. He wants me to have an abortion.

CLARISSA. That's for *you* to decide, not him.

EDIE. But he's the father ... And if I have a baby, my mother will throw me out.

CLARISSA. Look, honey, you a woman now. You gotta do whata *you* think's right ... Me? I had six kids, and I'd do it again. Gives you a brand new feelin' 'bout yourself, bein' a mother.

EDIE. You think so?

CLARISSA. I *knows* so ... Why, motherhood's the best thin' ever happened to me. Ain't nothin' in the world like it ... jes' you wait and see ...

EDIE. Nothing ... in the world?

CLARISSA. Nothing, darlin' ...

EDIE. Hm-m-mn ...

(CLARISSA rubs EDIE's shoulders and lightly strokes her hair. DOUG quietly appears upstage and watches them, unseen. The three form a tableau, as lights slowly fade.)

CURTAIN

COSTUME PLOT

CLARISSA:
> Cafeteria uniform or conservative blouse and skirt
> Butcher's apron
> Photo identification tag
> Comfortable shoes and stockings

EDIE:
> Mini-dress or mini-skirt and blouse
> Black tights and boots
> Boy's athletic jacket
> Multiple pieces of jewelry
> Bizarre hairstyle, gaudy makeup
> School bag
> Change purse

DOUG:
> Sweatsuit
> Athletic jacket
> White socks and sneakers
> Athletic bag
> Wallet

PROPERTY LIST

ONSTAGE:

Counter or long table with the following items:
> small cottage cheese container, small plastic box with simulated fruit, large plastic-wrapped cookie, small bags of chips and pretzels, candy bars and chewing gum, straws, paper napkins, tabloid newspaper.

Small stand or table with the following items:
> small juice and milk containers, Coca Cola and other soda cans, Styrofoam coffee cups and coffee pot (optional), cash box with bills and change.

Counter stool
Round cafe table with two chairs
Crumpled paper scattered on floor (for Clarissa to collect)

OFFSTAGE: (used by Clarissa when she re-enters):

> Small tray, paper towels, plastic trash bag

SET DRAWING

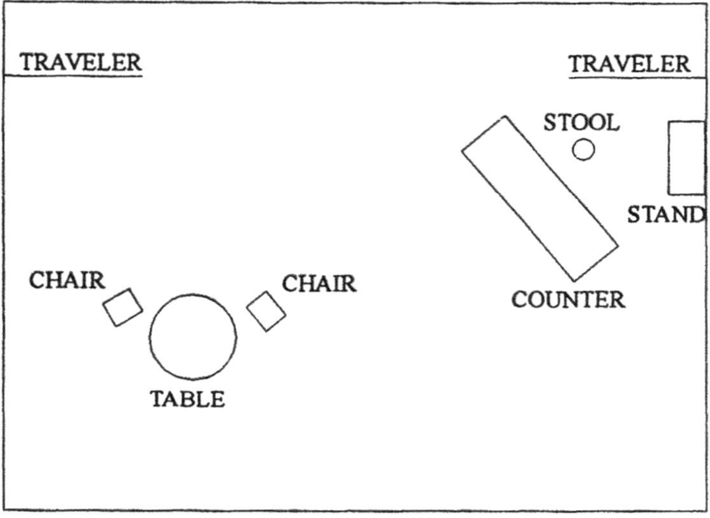

THE PRICE YOU PAY

by

Arlene Hutton

For Margot

THE PRICE YOU PAY
by
Arlene Hutton

with

MRS. ELDER . . . . Judith Hiller

MRS. YOUNGMAN . . . . Margot Avery

MAGGIE SPRINGFIELD . . . . Alana West

Directed by Beth Lincks

Presented by
The Journey Company

THE PRICE YOU PAY was presented by The Journey Company at the Edinburgh Festival Fringe in August, 1996, directed by Vivian Sorenson, with original music by Daniel J. Atkins. The cast included Margot Avery, Beth Lincks and Carla Cantrelle / Nancy Bell.

THE PRICE YOU PAY was restaged by The Journey Company at the Henry Street Settlement Experimental Space for the first New York International Fringe Festival, a production of The Present Company, August, 1997, directed by Beth Lincks with Lisa Hayes, Margot Avery and Stephanie Erb / Nanette DeWester.

ABOUT THE AUTHOR

ARLENE HUTTON is a member of New Dramatists and the recipient of a Cameron Mackinstosh Foundation grant. Her one-act *Studio Portrait* is published by Samuel French. Hutton's plays have been presented by The Journey Company at the Edinburgh Festival Fringe, and at theatres in New York and across the country. Her plays include *Last Train to Nibroc* and *I Dream Before I Take the Stand.* A member of the LAB Theatre Company and the Dramatists Guild, Arlene is represented by literary agent Donald Maass.

CHARACTERS

    MRS. ELDER: an upscale, smartly-dressed woman of fifty or sixty
    MRS. YOUNGMAN: not as bright, but very sweet, slightly younger,
        also well-dressed
    MAGGIE: Neatly dressed woman in her forties.

SETTING

    Place: A bench overlooking a fenced-in park
    Time: The present

(At lights up we see two smartly dressed women standing downstage facing the audience looking out. Behind them is a park bench.)

MRS. ELDER. *(Yelling at someone in front of her.)* Look at the birdy, Sammy!
MRS. YOUNGMAN. It's a big birdy! Billy! Watch it fly! Watch it –
MRS. ELDER. He didn't see it.
MRS. YOUNGMAN. Oh, yes he did. I'm sure he saw the bird.
MRS. ELDER. I don't think Billy saw it. Sammy saw it.
MRS. YOUNGMAN. I think he did, too. He likes birds. He looked up when it flew.
MRS. ELDER. That was because he heard your voice.
MRS. YOUNGMAN. He always turns when I speak. Billy does.
MRS. ELDER. Yes, that's so sweet.
MRS. YOUNGMAN. *(Calling to him.)* Billy! I'm here! I'm over here! Billy!
MRS. ELDER. He turned his head.
MRS. YOUNGMAN. He always does.
MRS. ELDER. I think he saw a bird.
MRS. YOUNGMAN. The other time. This time he heard my voice. Billy! See?
MRS. ELDER. Sammy!
MRS. YOUNGMAN. He didn't turn.

(MAGGIE has entered from upstage left. She stands upstage of the other women, staring out.)

MRS. ELDER. He sees the dog.
MRS. YOUNGMAN. Oh, yes. Billy, look at the doggie!
MRS. ELDER. Sammy, see the doggie? See the doggie run? Sammy!
MRS. YOUNGMAN. He sees it! They see it!

(MAGGIE sits on the left side of the bench.)

MRS. ELDER. He's smiling. Look at him smile. Smile, Sammy! See the dog?
MRS. YOUNGMAN. Billy! See the dog! Woof, woof!
MRS. ELDER. Sammy! Watch the –
MRS. YOUNGMAN. *(Standing)* That's so sweet! Look at them!
MRS. ELDER. What's a dog doing there?
MRS. YOUNGMAN. I don't know.

MRS. ELDER. There's never been a dog here before.
MRS. YOUNGMAN. Really? Are you sure?
MRS. ELDER. Never. Not in all the years.
MRS. YOUNGMAN. A dog is nice to –
MRS. ELDER. I've never seen a dog before. Not here.

(MRS. ELDER sits on the right side of the bench.)

MRS. YOUNGMAN. Whose is it?

(She starts to sit down on MAGGIE's sandwich.)

MAGGIE. Oh, wait, my –
MRS. YOUNGMAN. What?
MAGGIE. My lunch.
MRS. YOUNGMAN. Oh! I'm sorry.

(MRS. YOUNGMAN sits in the middle of the park bench, between MRS. ELDER and MAGGIE.)

MAGGIE. No, I'm sorry. It's new.
MRS. YOUNGMAN. Excuse me?
MAGGIE. They said it's new. The dog.
MRS. ELDER. *(Pointing out.)* And your, uh, which?
MAGGIE. In the blue shirt.
MRS. ELDER. Yes, I thought he was new.
MAGGIE. The dog's a new thing.
MRS. YOUNGMAN. What for?
MAGGIE. The nurses said.
MRS. ELDER. It's a good idea. They're all smiling.
MAGGIE. Yes. Pet therapy.
MRS. YOUNGMAN. They look happy. They see the dog.
MAGGIE. Yes. It's pet therapy.
MRS. ELDER. I'm Elizabeth Elder. Sammy's in the yellow shirt and khaki pants.
MAGGIE. Oh, yes. Sammy. I'm Maggie. Maggie Springfield. Jim is –
MRS. ELDER. Nice to meet you.
MAGGIE. Yes. And you.
MRS. YOUNGMAN. Nice to have you –
MRS. ELDER. Sammy, say hello to Jimmy! His chair's facing the wrong way.
MAGGIE. Jim.
MRS. ELDER. *(To someone out front.)* Sammy's wheelchair's facing the wrong way.
MRS. YOUNGMAN. *(Loudly, facing front.)* Billy, that's Jimmy!
MAGGIE. Uh, Jim.

MRS. YOUNGMAN. Oh, they see each other! The nurse moved his chair! They see each other! How nice!

MAGGIE. How long have – *(They look at her.)* I mean ... *(Beat)* It's nice here.

MRS. ELDER. It's very –

MRS. YOUNGMAN. Nice.

MAGGIE. Pretty.

MRS. YOUNGMAN. We're very lucky.

MAGGIE. Lucky?

MRS. YOUNGMAN. It's such a nice place for them.

MAGGIE. It's very pretty here.

MRS. YOUNGMAN. It's nice to have you here.

MAGGIE. Thank you.

(Pause)

MRS. ELDER. What can yours do?

MAGGIE. Do?

MRS. ELDER. Well, he doesn't read.

MAGGIE. No, he doesn't.

MRS. YOUNGMAN. Billy looks at magazines.

MAGGIE. Jim likes jigsaw puzzles.

MRS. ELDER. Jigsaw puzzles?

MAGGIE. He likes those.

MRS. YOUNGMAN. Really?

MAGGIE. Well, small ones.

MRS. ELDER. He doesn't work them.

MAGGIE. He tries to. He tries to work jigsaw puzzles. He always enjoyed –

MRS. ELDER. Really.

MAGGIE. Um, how long –

MRS. ELDER. Why do you ask?

MAGGIE. *(Giving up.)* Conversation.

MRS. ELDER. Really?

MRS. YOUNGMAN. Your Jimmy isn't as old as –

MRS. ELDER. Jimmy's not as old as my Sammy. Or Billy.

MAGGIE. No, he's not.

MRS. ELDER. Then he'll be here longer.

MAGGIE. I guess.

MRS. YOUNGER. Longer.

MAGGIE. Probably. They don't know.

MRS. ELDER. They never know.

MRS. YOUNGMAN. Billy's been here –

MRS. ELDER. It's the price you pay.

MAGGIE. Excuse me?

MRS. YOUNGMAN. They have him in a chair already?

MAGGIE. He wanders.

MRS. ELDER. Of course.

MAGGIE. And he falls.

MRS. ELDER. *(Standing and moving behind the bench.)* The price you pay. For marrying an older man. We all pay. We get the house and the car and all the clothes and the travel and the country club –

MAGGIE. I don't belong to –

MRS. ELDER. *(Standing at MAGGIE's left.)* All the money. We don't have to go through those early years of debt. You married an older man.

MAGGIE. Yes.

MRS. ELDER. *(Pointing out.)* And there he is. Your husband. It's the price you pay.

MAGGIE. It could have been anything.

MRS. ELDER. He's what, twenty, thirty years older? *(Looking out.)* Look at them. Sam there is thirty-two years older than I am. Already CEO when I met him. I was twenty-five. A stewardess. Twenty-five. It's the price you pay. You get the fancy house and the designer clothes and the fur coats. You get them while you're young and still look good in them. No waiting. You don't have to wait. You get it all. You get it all fast. You even get to keep it. But there's a price.

MAGGIE. I don't see it that way. I married him because I loved –

MRS. ELDER. You're paying the price.

MRS. YOUNGMAN. They got two lives. One before you and one with you. Two good lives. You only get one life with them and then this one now.

MRS. ELDER. That's the price.

MRS. YOUNGMAN. Bill was a neurosurgeon. Oh, he's looking at the squirrel! *(She stands up.)* Billy, see the squirrel. *(Walking downstage right to see better.)* Oh, they're looking at the squirrel!

MRS. ELDER. *(Takes a few steps downstage left.)* Sammy! See the squirrels! Look!

MAGGIE. *(Standing and coming downstage a bit. She is between the other two women.)* There's a black squirrel.

(All the women are facing out. The following dialog overlaps just ever so slightly.)

MRS. YOUNGMAN. Oh, yes! I've never seen that one before –

MRS. ELDER. Sammy, look at the black squirrel! Watch the squirrel!

MAGGIE. He's by Jim. He's running up the tree –

MRS. YOUNGMAN. Jimmy, look at the squirrel!

MRS. ELDER. He's looking right at –

MAGGIE. Jimmy, honey, look at the squirrel!

MRS. YOUNGMAN. That's so cute!

MAGGIE. He's smiling.
MRS. ELDER. Look, there's the dog –
MRS. YOUNGMAN. The dog's chasing the squirrels! Oh! Billy! Watch the doggie!
MRS. ELDER. Look at the squirrels run up the –
MAGGIE. Jimmy! Watch the black squirrel. Don't let the dog get him!
MRS. YOUNGMAN. Billy! Oh, good, Billy! He turned his head!
MRS. ELDER. Sammy! Sammy's smiling, too. Good, Sammy –
MAGGIE. Jimmy! Watch the black squirrel. He's teasing the dog! Jimmy! Watch the squirrel!
MRS. ELDER. Good, Jimmy!
MRS. YOUNGMAN. Jimmy! Look at them! Oh, this is fun!

(MAGGIE stares at first one woman and then the other. She thinks.)

MRS. ELDER. Watch the dog!
MRS. YOUNGMAN. We always had dogs. Billy likes dogs. This is such fun!
MAGGIE. *(Gathering her sandwich stuff from the bench.)* I have to go.
MRS. YOUNGMAN. *(Pointing up right.)* The restroom's –
MAGGIE. I have to leave.
MRS. YOUNGMAN. But the dog is such fun.
MAGGIE. Nice meeting you. Really.
MRS. ELDER. Sammy! Say good-bye to ...
MAGGIE. *(To MRS. ELDER.)* Maggie. *(Looking out.)* I'm Maggie.
MRS. YOUNGMAN. *(Waving out front.)* Billy! Say bye-bye to –

(She turns to MAGGIE.)

MAGGIE. *(Looking out.)* Good-bye, Jim. I have to say goodbye.
MRS. ELDER. *(To MAGGIE.)* See you next week.
MAGGIE. *(To MRS. ELDER.)* No. I won't be back. But thank you.
MRS. ELDER. Of course you'll be back.
MAGGIE. *(She looks out.)* I promised Jim –
MRS. ELDER. Promised him what?
MAGGIE. – that I wouldn't come. Early on, when we knew, when he could still ... I promised him.
MRS. YOUNGMAN. It should still be nice next week.
MRS. ELDER. Promised what?
MRS. YOUNGMAN. The weather. Nice.
MAGGIE. That I wouldn't come see him. That I'd get on with –
MRS. YOUNGMAN. It's so nice here.
MAGGIE. Get on with my life.
MRS. ELDER. But you're here.

MAGGIE. I broke my promise. I shouldn't have. He was right. Eve
then he knew.

MRS. YOUNGMAN. But it's very nice here.

MAGGIE. Yes, it is. I'm glad he's here. But I won't be back.

MRS. ELDER. Yes, you will. You have to –

MAGGIE. Pay a price? Yes, you're right. But I won't be back.

MRS. YOUNGMAN. You're never going to see him again?

MAGGIE. That's the price.

MRS. ELDER. What price?

MAGGIE. The price I pay for making a promise. The price is that
have to keep it. The promise.

MRS. YOUNGMAN. *(She goes to sit back on the bench.)* Mayb
you'll change your –

MAGGIE. I won't be back.

*(MAGGIE stands upstage left looking out front. MRS. ELDER sits on th
bench next to MRS. YOUNGMAN. They both are looking ou
defeated.)*

MRS. ELDER. *(Without her earlier energy.)* Sammy sees the do
again. Sammy, watch the dog chase the squirrels.

MRS. YOUNGMAN. *(Looking out.)* Where did the black squirrel go

MRS. ELDER. I don't know. I didn't see him. Billy, where's the blac
squirrel?

MAGGIE. It went over the fence. It's gone.

(MAGGIE exits.)
(Blackout)

END OF PLAY

COSTUME PLOT

MRS. ELDER:
    A very expensive pants suit in beige or brown tones
    Expensive jewelry
    Expensive wedding ring set
    Optional scarf
    Brown or beige pumps

MRS. YOUNGMAN:
    A very expensive pants suit or skirt suit in brown
    Expensive wedding ring
    Scarf (if Mrs. Elder is wearing one)
    Brown or beige pumps

MAGGIE:
    Black print skirt
    Light-colored top
    Black or dark grey sweater
    Black boots or shoes
    Optional scarf

PROPERTY LIST

Maggie:

    Brown paper bag containing a sandwich
    Purse or shoulder bag

SET

A park bench, big enough for three

PEARLS

by

Nira Lipner

To my mother, Ima,
with love and gratitude

PEARLS
by
Nira Lipner

with

RUTH . . . . Lucille Patton

MARINA . . . . Alice Rosengard

Directed by Roger Hendricks Simon
Original music by Howard Levitsky

Presented by
The Simon Studio

ABOUT THE AUTHOR

NIRA LIPNER is a lucky survivor of a long career in advertising. *Pearls* was produced by the Heartlande Theatre Co. in Michigan (1998). *Just Women* was produced by The Simon Studio at the Greenwich Street Theatre (1998) and was a finalist in the 1998 Open Book National Playwrighting Contest and in the Perishable Theatre Annual Women's Playwrighting Festival. *So Beautiful* was performed at the Pulse Theatre in NYC (1999).

CHARACTERS

> RUTH: A widow in her mid-sixties, or older.
> MARINE: A woman in her mid-fifties.

SETTING

> Place: Ruth's living room
> Time: The present

MARINA. Hello dear. Sorry I'm late. (They embrace in a formal manner.) Took the wrong bus and couldn't figure out where I was.
RUTH. Well Marina, that's for getting her so rarely.
MARINA. Busses run both ways.
RUTH. It is customary, that the widow is the one to receive visitors, not the other way around.
MARINA. Seven years later? How long do you think an active state of widowhood should last?
RUTH. For the rest of my life. After a union like ours.
MARINA. It's over seven years already.
RUTH. You think I don't know?
MARINA. I was surprised you called.
RUTH. I saw you at the firm last week.
MARINA. I know. You were there to ...
RUTH. Go over my will.
MARINA. I watched you through the glass door.
RUTH. I saw you watching me.
MARINA. I was happy you called.
RUTH. Won't you sit down, please?
MARINA. Thank you. (Pause) You called. After all this time.
RUTH. They told me about your retirement.
MARINA. Yes. December thirty first.
RUTH. They made you do it.
MARINA. They gave me a good deal.
RUTH. Of course they did. They had to. They don't do anything they don't have to. Why didn't you fight them?
MARINA. What's the use? Can't fight natural cycles.
RUTH. Natural cycles ...
MARINA. Well Ruth, this is how it goes. First you're a brilliant young ...
RUTH. Attractive. (Pause) Attractive.
MARINA. First you're a young attractive brilliant woman lawyer. Then you're a brilliant woman lawyer. Then you're a woman lawyer. Then you're just a woman.
RUTH. Just a woman.
MARINA. An older woman.

RUTH. That's what I felt when I saw you there. Me going over m
will. You going into retirement. Two older woman. Just women. An
I felt ...

(Pause)

MARINA. What?
RUTH. I don't know much about baseball but I think you woul
understand if I describe it as the bottom of the ninth, the score is tied an
the count is three and two ...
MARINA. Who's at bat?
RUTH. A couple of days after I saw you, my daughter, my Joanna
came to me in distress and there I was. My brilliant independent daughte
came to me and I was there. *(Pause)* Who's at bat? I'm at bat. For the firs
time in my life, I realized that it's me. I'm the bat.
MARINA. That's when you called.
RUTH. Yes. And here we are.
MARINA. *(Pause)* I like your earrings.
RUTH. I remember you always liked them. You used to admire then
whenever I wore them.
MARINA. They're beautiful. Sapphire beads surrounded with fresl
water pearls. *(Pause)* But I remember you rather liked cultured pearls.
RUTH. Yes, and it was you who preferred fresh water pearls.
MARINA. You're right. I still do.
RUTH. *(Long pause.)* I was going to have lunch ready for us, but I go
distracted. The pictures ... so many memories. Love, pain – a marriage.
don't know how much you understand. You can't.
MARINA. But here I am.
RUTH. After all this time.
MARINA. Yes.
RUTH. It's such an occasion, I thought we would have a ... sort of
memorial service.
MARINA. That's why all these pictures.
RUTH. Yes, all these pictures.
MARINA. They span a life.
RUTH. And what a life.
MARINA. I keep looking at this one.
RUTH. Which one?
MARINA. This one here. You can see the triumph in the eyes. The
look of a hunter back with the prey. I told him I used to see this look in my
cat's eyes when she came in from the garden with a mouse in her mouth.
RUTH. How did he like this comparison?
MARINA. He laughed. He liked it. *(Pause)* He certainly had
something to celebrate. This was right after he won the larges
conglomerate takeover case.
RUTH. I remember that case. Was right after New Year's. The firs

case of the year. Was a nice way to start the year. Strange ... he looks tanned. We didn't go away that Christmas. I remember, because Jeremy had the mumps.

MARINA. Of course he was tanned, this was in the Bahamas. A celebration weekend.

RUTH. A celebration weekend in the Bahamas ... my memory must be going. *(Long pause.)* You're looking at my earrings again.

MARINA. They're beautiful.

RUTH. Jack gave them to me. Jack liked to buy presents. Everything I have was a present from Jack for one occasion or another. I still haven't learned to buy things for myself.

MARINA. Maybe you should.

RUTH. Yes, I should. It's funny, you know ...

MARINA. What's funny?

RUTH. Me saying I should learn to buy things for myself.

MARINA. Why is it funny?

RUTH. A reversal. I remember when you bought your fur coat. You got a coat almost exactly like mine. Jack sent you to the furrier where we bought all my coats. He must have given you a real good deal. I felt so bad for you. A woman buying her own fur coat. *(Pause)* My Joanna thinks it's an insult to accept a fur coat from a man.

MARINA. Joanna is brilliant.

RUTH. Yes. She is. She's a young, attractive, brilliant woman lawyer.

MARINA. Times change, Ruth. Women have changed.

RUTH. Some things don't change. *(No response.)* No one can understand the kind of relationship Jack and I had. The depth. The devotion. Jack worshiped the ground I walked on. *(No response.)* I don't have to tell you.

MARINE. What?

RUTH. How much Jack loved me. *(No response.)* Everybody knew that. *(No response.)* Look at this picture. This was at Jeremy's wedding. What a gorgeous affair it was. Jack sat back and looked at the family we created. He turned to me. It wasn't the hunter's look I saw in his face. He had tears in his eyes. He held me by the shoulders and said: "Thank you Ruth. Thank you. Thank you for everything. And I'm sorry." That's what he said. "What are you sorry for," I said, "it was a wonderful life." But by then I was crying too. *(Pause)* Listen to me going on and on. How much any of this means to you, I don't know. *(No response.)* You lived your life alone.

MARINA. Single.

RUTH. A woman alone.

MARINA. A free woman.

RUTH. No one to take care of you.

MARINA. Independent.

RUTH. No one to take care of.

MARINA. Liberated.

RUTH. No children.

MARINA. No children.

RUTH. Sex?

MARINA. Sex.

RUTH. Often?

MARINA. It depended ...

RUTH. On?

MARINA. I took what I could get.

RUTH. Good?

MARINA. Sometimes.

RUTH. *(Long pause.)* You know, I wonder, why would Jack buy fresh water pearls when he knew how much I liked cultured pearls.

MARINA. Did you ask him?

RUTH. That summer the kids were in camp and Jack was in some legal conference. I felt terribly alone. I decided to surprise him. I think you were in the same conference. I remember that, because I was surprised to see you there. It was supposed to be a partners' conference. *(Pause)* There were no women partners yet. Why were you there?

MARINA. Probably some project Jack and I were working on. How can I remember all these years back.

RUTH. Jack always admired your brain. I could have become jealous, you know. Good thing our marriage was so solid.

MARINA. It was ...

RUTH. When I came to Jack's room, there were these earrings, just sitting on his dresser. He didn't know I was coming and didn't even wrap them yet. I wasn't surprised because wherever he went Jack always got something for me. He said he thought of me when he saw these earrings because the sapphires looked like our babies' blue eyes and the pearls ...

MARINA. Like your babies' teeth?

RUTH. Yes, that's what he said.

MARINA. To me the sapphires look like the eyes of unborn babies, and the pearls like the teeth they could have had.

RUTH. You have the imagination of an unborn mother.

MARINA. *(Pause)* Of an unborn wife.

RUTH. *(Long pause.)* Should I feel sorry for you?

MARINA. Don't.

RUTH. I wanted to hurt you.

MARINA. And you don't?

RUTH. Not anymore. My Joanna is very much like you.

MARINA. Not exactly. *(Pause)* I didn't buy my fur coat.

RUTH. I know. *(Pause)* Here I am, at bat, and all of a sudden I don't really know what would actually be a win ... I don't know how to play this game. *(Pause)* What do I do next?

MARINA. How about some lunch for starters?

RUTH. All I have in the refrigerator is a washed out chicken.

MARINA. Washed out chicken?

RUTH. You take a plump beautiful spring chicken. It makes wonderful soup. Then what do you have left? A squeezed out, dried out, wrung out piece of flesh.

MARINA. And what if that chicken were not made into soup? Just left to grow to old age?

RUTH. She would become an old chicken. Soft muscles, hard flesh. *(Pause)* Cooked chicken is at least soft. With lots of mayonnaise it can still make a good dish.

MARINA. *(Pause)* Remember Matthew Walters?

RUTH. He was one of the partners. His wife died before ... I met him at the last Christmas party.

MARINA. He asked about you.

RUTH. That's nice.

MARINA. He's interested.

RUTH. I'm not a spring chicken any more.

MARINA. Well, with lots of mayonnaise ...

RUTH. That's crude. A man's joke. You spent your life with men. *(Pause)* After Jack started working with you, he said one day, here is a woman you can spend a lifetime with. She jokes, she drinks, she plays ball, she fights, she laughs, she has guts.

MARINA. That was cruel.

RUTH. Yes. But they never married women like you. Fools. *(Pause)* We'll have lunch. I'll make chicken salad sandwiches.

MARINA. That's not what I want.

RUTH. What is it that you want? I don't have much else.

MARINA. Recognition. I want recognition.

RUTH. You want recognition?

MARINA. Yes.

RUTH. You want recognition.

MARINA. Yes. That's what I want.

RUTH. You won't be happy with chicken salad?

MARINA. You're still angry.

RUTH. No, I'm not angry. I just ache.

MARINA. Ache?

RUTH. It was a movie I watched late one night. There was this scene, an after sex moment. They were just lying there. And then, with his finger, he traced a perspiration bead that was trickling down her neck. He didn't touch it, just slowly moved his finger alongside it. Such a simple gesture. My legs started trembling. I was aching. I felt tremors running through my body. I cried and I yelled out into the empty bedroom: fuck you Jack. *Fuck you. (Long pause. RUTH wipes off tears. MARINA walks over to RUTH. They embrace. MARINA strokes RUTH's hair. After a couple of minutes RUTH straightens up, takes off her earrings and gives them to MARINA. Long pause.)* Tell Matthew Walters he can call me.

END

COSTUME PLOT

RUTH:
> Upper-class, tailored clothes:
>> Long sleeve blouse, Pants, Scarf, Low shoes, Earrings (pearls surrounding blue stone/stones/beads), Pearl necklace

MARINA:
> Lawyer's business suit:
>> Blouse, Dark jacket, Matching skirt, Medium heel shoes

PROPERTY PLOT

Two Straight-back Chairs
> One left of C.
> One right of C.
> Set approximately four feet apart, angled to audience and each other.

Earrings
> Pearls surrounding blue stone/stones/beads.

Though pictures on a wall are referred to in the dialogue, they were placed on the fourth wall in the original production.

OPHELIA

by

Karen Sanford

For

Fele Bannon

Myrtis Saulters

and

Annie Lou Sanford

OPHELIA
by
Karen Sanford

with

FELIE . . . . Jennie Epland

BILLY WILSON . . . . Jason McDermot

Directed by Wally Strauss

Presented by
The HomeGrown Theatre

ABOUT THE AUTHOR

KAREN SANFORD is a playwright and actor born and reared in Mississippi and a graduate of the University of Southern Mississippi. *Ophelia* is her second play. Other one-act plays produced in New York include *Kiss, Strip, Confessions of A Businessman,* and *Daughterland.* She is a member of the Dramatists Guild and lives in New York City.

CHARACTERS

> OPHELIA: 13 years old
> BILLY WILSON: 38 years old

SETTING

> Place: Rural South Mississippi. The front yard of Ophelia's house.
> Time: A scorching, hot August afternoon.

(At rise there is only the sound of the ebb and flow of summer cicadas. Lights up first on FELIE stage left tossing a softball up and catching it with a tattered glove. She sings to herself "The Old Rugged Cross." A bench is placed down center. Lights up on BILLY upstage right watching FELIE. She drops the ball when BILLY speaks.)

FELIE. *"On a hill far away, stood an old rugged cross –"*
BILLY. That's a mighty pretty song you're singing. *(She runs away.)* Hey! Wait. Come here. I want to ask you something. Hey, I don't want to have to scream at you. Come over here so I can talk to you. *(She walks over, but not too close.)* That's better. Is Tom here?
FELIE. No. He's not here.
BILLY. He's not. *(She runs away.)* Hey come here. *(Cautiously stepping back.)* When do you reckon he'll be back?
FELIE. He's at work. He works on Saturdays. He should be in soon, though.
BILLY. Well, I just wanted to come by and see him. Hadn't seen him in years, thought I'd stop by. *(She runs away.)* Hey, stop running off. What are you scared of? I don't bite. At least not hard. *(Inching back to him.)* So, you say he'll be here soon? How soon is soon? I need to get my truck looked at.
FELIE. Not long.
BILLY. Not long? Is that twenty minutes or two hours?
FELIE. I don't know.
BILLY. Who are you?
FELIE. I'm Tom's daughter.
BILLY. You ain't his daughter. Last time I saw you, you weren't knee-high to a grasshopper. From what I remember of Tom, you're too pretty to be his daughter.
FELIE. Well ...
BILLY. I'm Billy Wilson. What's your name girl?

(Holding out his hand.)

FELIE. Felie. *(Shakes his hand.)* My real name is Ophelia. I think it comes from the Bible. But people think it's too fancy, so they just call me Felie.
BILLY. And how old are you, Felie?
FELIE. Thirteen.
BILLY. Thirteen, that's big. *(He sits on bench.)* I can't get over how pretty you are. You must have a hundred boyfriends. Tom must have to

keep extra shotguns around the house just to run off all the boys lined up at the front door.

FELIE. No, that is not true.

BILLY. What? That he don't keep shotguns here or that boys don't think you're pretty? *(Beat)* Aw! I didn't mean to hurt your feelings. Come on, you must know how pretty you are. You're like a wood nymph. You know what that is? It's the spirit of a beautiful, young girl that haunts the woods. Innocent and wild, exciting the hell out of everything she touches.

FELIE. ... Um, I don't know anything about that, but I wish you wouldn't cuss in front of me. I don't appreciate it.

BILLY. What are you talking about? Cuss? What'd I say? ... Oh, you mean hell. Hell, hell, ain't no cuss word. It's a geographic location. A place they say I'm goin'. The more I think about it, the more I think they're probably right.

FELIE. Well, whoever told you that may be right, unless you accept The Lord Jesus Christ as your Savior.

BILLY. Oh, well, ma'am, you may be right about that.

FELIE. I am right.

BILLY. Oh, I bet you are!

FELIE. Betting is a sin.

BILLY. Well, you got me good, hadn't you. I better get my ass ... self in church before I say anything else. *(He gets up to leave but stops to watch FELIE pick up the softball.)* I just can't get over how pretty you are. You, uh ... you think I could take you out sometime?

FELIE. No!

BILLY. Don't be so mean. I'll get all dressed up. I'll even take a bath. We'll go over to Johnny's Fish Camp. On Saturday nights they got all-you-can-eat catfish for eight dollars a head.

FELIE. I been there before.

BILLY. That's a nice place, ain't it?

FELIE. I can't go back to that restaurant.

BILLY. Sure you can. I'll drive you.

FELIE. No. *(She sits.)* I went one time with Mama and Daddy and my brothers. And they gave us so much fish, my Mama hated to see it waste, so she wrapped some up in some napkins to take home for us.

BILLY. She's a smart woman. See even your Mama likes it, so there ain't no reason in the world why you shouldn't go out there with me and eat dinner.

FELIE. The waitress got mad at Mama cause I don't think you were supposed to take any food that you couldn't eat, and she caught Mama putting a piece of that catfish in her purse. Mama started fighting with her, mainly cause she was embarrassed, and they told us not to come back again.

BILLY. Well, I'll tell you what: we'll go to a different restaurant. How's that?

FELIE. I don't date unsaved boys.

BILLY. Felie, I don't know if you've noticed, but I'm not a boy, I'm much –
FELIE. I know. You're old.
BILLY. I'm older than you. Guess how old I am.

(Stepping back to give her a better look.)

FELIE. I don't know. Twenty?
BILLY. That's pretty close. In the old days, girls were already married at your age. *(Circling behind her.)* Anyway, we're getting ahead of ourselves – I ain't asking you to marry me. I just want to take you out. *(Touching her hair.)* We'll have fun.
FELIE. I don't ... I don't think so. I better go in the house. My mama is looking out the window.

(Pointing down right.)

BILLY. I don't see her. *(She runs away.)* Wait a minute. Come back here. You run faster than a jackrabbit. Come over here and talk to me. *(He sits and motions for her to sit with him – she looks away and he stands to offer her the bench alone. She sits.)* Your Mama, she never lets you have any fun does she?
FELIE. No, not much.
BILLY. I bet – I mean, does she make you clean up your room?
FELIE. Clean up my room? She makes me work in the garden and wash dishes and clean up the whole house. My brothers never have to work. I hate them.
BILLY. That's a downright shame. That is not right. I'm gonna have to do something about this. As soon as your Daddy gets home and looks at my truck, I'll be ready to go. We won't say nothing to your Mama and Daddy. You'll just hop in the truck with me, and we'll go have ourselves a good time. I'll even stop off and buy you a dress so's you don't look like a boy.
FELIE. I have a dress. I have three dresses, and I don't look like a boy. And, anyway, I can't go out with you. I – there's no church tonight, and that's the only place I could go with you.
BILLY. Who said?
FELIE. God said, that's who. I can't go out with boys – anybody who is not saved.
BILLY. We'll find a church. Hey, I got an idea. We'll go off somewhere and make our own church. I'll tell you all about my sinful life, and I'll let you be the preacher. You can save me.
FELIE. Girls can't be preachers.
BILLY,. Felie. Felie. Don't fight me on this. *(Sitting on bench, pulling her close to him.)* You are so pretty. You don't deserve to be thrown out of

restaurants and worked like a slave. I'll treat you like a queen. Ophelia, the Wood Nymph, Queen of the Woods. I'll treat you like a lady, a grown-up lady. I'll open the door for you and pull out your chair. You can eat as much as you want and leave food on your plate if you want to. Listen, I don't have time to wait for your Daddy. I'll get my truck fixed on the road. You come go with me right now, and we'll have a real good time.

FELIE. *(Breaking away from him.)* Stop saying that. This is not right. You're too old and you don't even know me. The Bible says I have to abstain from all appearance of evil, and I think —

BILLY. *(Rising)* You think I'm evil? I tell you you're pretty, and your Mama makes you work like a dog and won't let you do anything, and I'm evil?

FELIE. I don't know. *(Beat)* No.

BILLY. Felie. *(He goes to touch her face — she recoils as if being slapped.)* What'd I do? I wasn't gonna hit you. You poor, sweet girl. *(She backs away.)* I'm not evil. Whoever hits you is evil. I've done bad things, but I'm not evil.

(He sits on the bench with head in hands.)

FELIE. It don't matter if you've done bad things. "God sent his only begotten Son, that whosoever believeth in Him should not perish but have everlasting life." God forgives you for everything you've ever done that's bad. It's all washed away as if you never did it.

BILLY. Who said what I've done is bad?

FELIE. We're all bad. We can't help it.

BILLY. That's right, Felie. We can't help it.

(Turning to leave.)

FELIE. Hey, where're you going?

BILLY. You better get in the house, Felie. Didn't your mean Mama tell you not to talk to strangers?

FELIE. If you want to go to church on Sunday, I'll go with you. You can pick me up. And I'll wear a dress. *(He turns to go.)* Hey! *(Giggling with embarrassment.)* Bye.

BILLY. Goodbye, Ophelia.

(Lights dim and spotlight on BILLY while FELIE sings two bars of "The Old Rugged Cross", then begins humming softly the remainder of the song walking in hesitated steps as if in a funeral march. BILLY speaks when she begins humming.)

FELIE. *"On a hill far away, stood an old rugged cross, the emblem of suffering and shame."* ...

BILLY. I was traveling through Oklahoma. Actually, I was running through Oklahoma. The cops were after me for picking up this nine year-old girl. I was just having some fun with her. But I messed up. I needed some money and had no way to get it. It was late at night, like one o'clock in the morning and I thought ... I thought I might break into this house I kept passing. I parked the truck and snuck around to the back door. It was open. I tiptoed in and felt my way around. I was trying to get to the bedroom, maybe go through a wallet, grab some jewelry, and at the entry to the bedroom, I saw a small light blast from a gun shooting off. Unfortunately, the woman in the bed was a helluva good shot, and she got me right in the stomach. I didn't die right away. I heard her screaming and calling the cops, and all I could think about was that hot, sunny day and that girl with the strange name trying to save me.

(Lights dim on BILLY and spot on FELIE centerstage.)

FELIE. I got a call from the woman at the church that does all the music, and she told me I had to sing at a funeral. It was on a Tuesday during the day when everybody else who sings in the church was working, and since it wasn't a big member of the community and just a graveside funeral, she asked me to do it. She told me to sing "The Old Rugged Cross." She wouldn't tell me who died – like it was some big secret. There were only four people at the funeral – alive that is. Me, the preacher, and the dead man's parents. None of them cried. I've been to so many funerals that I never cry, but you would think these two old people would. Usually the preacher talks about how the person dead is already in heaven and the family should be happy, but he didn't say that this time. He sort of wished the dead guy best of luck. It was cold that day, and I was wearing a thin dress with no hose. I was really shaking. But I sang. For some reason I was really scared -- not for singing in front of people. Like I said, I do that all the time. But, there was something scary about this coffin going into the ground and nobody caring. After it was over, the preacher drove me home, and he told me who we had just buried and what he had done to a little girl in Oklahoma, and that's why nobody was at the funeral. *(Beat)* I couldn't speak. I knew who he was. He was that man that had come to the house. They should have told me before ... before I sang. They didn't know I knew him, but they should have told me. I really think they should have told me who he was.

(Lights fade.)

COSTUME PLOT

OPHELIA:
    Long denim cut-off shorts
    Old t-shirt or button down sleeveless shirt
    Dirty sneakers (or barefoot)

BILLY WILSON:
    Blue jeans
    White t-shirt
    Boots

PROPERTY PLOT

Ophelia:
    Softball glove
    Softball

GROUND PLAN

Bare stage with small wooden bench (no back)

The Old Rugged Cross

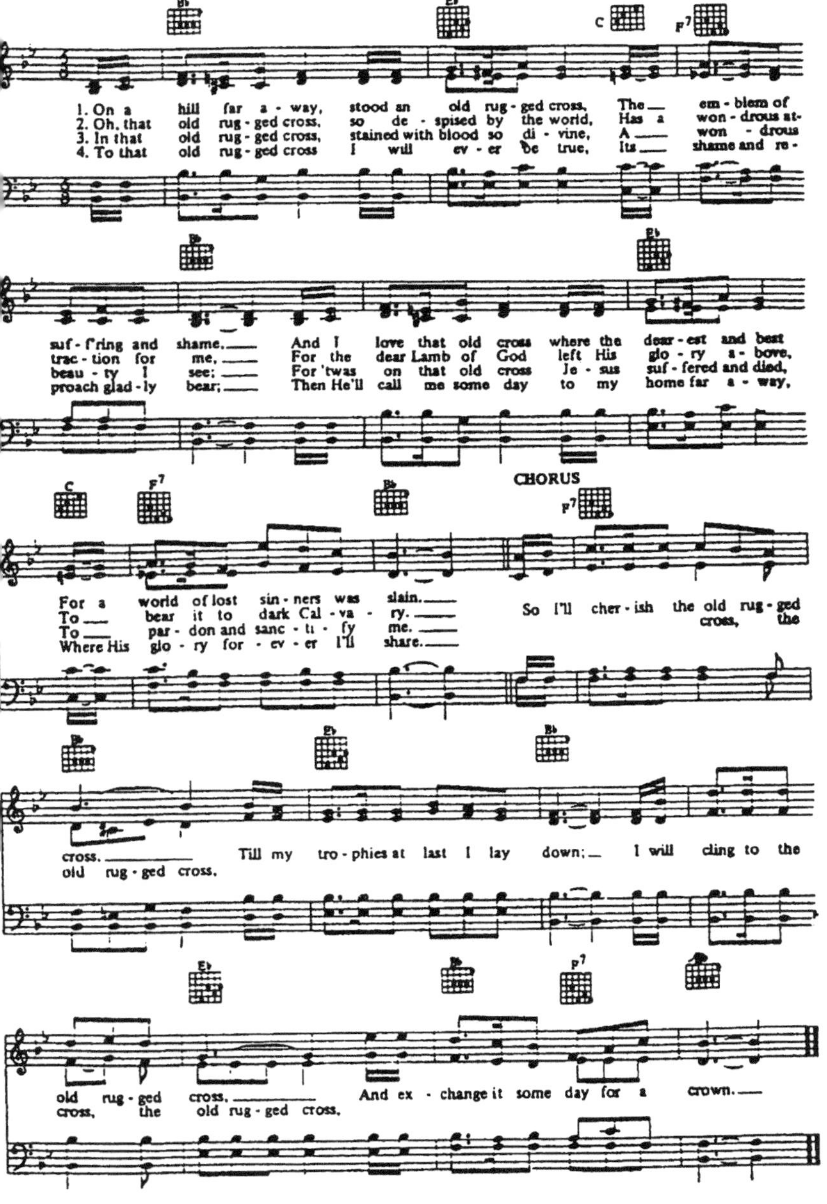

A SIGNIFICANT BETRAYAL

by

Le Wilhelm

To William Talbot

A SIGNIFICANT BETRAYAL
by
Le Wilhelm

with

DORRY . . . . Beth LaGrange

ASA . . . . Sam Street

Directed by Sharon Fallon

Presented by
Love Creek Productions

ABOUT THE AUTHOR

Born and raised in the Missouri Ozarks, Le Wilhelm has had countless productions in cities all over the world, including a Los Angeles production of *Cucumbers* and an Italian-language production of *The Missouri Trilogy* in Rome. Among his plays published by Samuel French, Inc. are *Strawberry Preserves, The Power and the Glory, Cherry Blend with Vanilla, Life Comes to the Old Maid, Tremulous,* and *Meridian Mississippi Redux,* the companion piece to *A Significant Betrayal.* The full-length *Missouri Trilogy,* consisting of *Pie Supper, One-Eyed Venus and the Brothers* and *Blackberry Frost,* is also represented by Samuel French.

CHARACTERS

    DORRY: an unassuming young woman
    ASA: her uncle

SETTING

    Place: A swamp
    Time: The present

On stage we see a man around 50. Not in the best of shape, not very well kept, working on an old piece of furniture. Because this could be difficult I will describe what I have in mind knowing that the director will choose to do as he/she sees fit. The piece of furniture could be a chair or deacon's bench type structure. It should look very old. What the man is doing is trying to glue the piece of furniture back together. His efforts at restoring the piece should have a certain professionalism about them. However, we should not feel that he is a past master at this job.)

ASA fits a piece of wood into place after having glued it in the appropriate place. He wipes sweat from his face. Works some more. After awhile, we hear a car. ASA looks up. The car approaches. The engine shuts off. A door slams. ASA watches but does not wave or move toward what is obviously the approaching person.)

The person, a young woman. comes into view. She is somewhere past 18 but certainly not 30. She is dressed conservatively. She is dressed in feminine colors. She would be considered attractive by most people.)

He looks at her, says nothing.)

DORRY. *(After a time, smiling.)* Hello.
ASA. Mmh.

Back to work.)

DORRY. Uncle Asa, right?
ASA. Asa's my name, all right.
DORRY. You know me, don't you?
ASA. *(Pause)* Annie's daughter, I reckon.
DORRY. That's right.
ASA. Dorothea.
DORRY. Dorry.
ASA. You prefer being called Dorry instead of Dorothea.
DORRY. *(Smiling for real.)* What do you think?
ASA. I can see your point. *(As he goes back to work an awkward ilence passes.)* So what brought my sister's daughter out here to the wamp?
DORRY. I came to see you.
ASA. Mmh.
DORRY. I seldom see you.
ASA. And to what do I owe this sudden visitation?

DORRY. *(Beginning to understand this isn't going to be easy.)* N
particular –
ASA. Someone die?
DORRY. *(Laughs in spite of herself.)* No.
ASA. You think death is funny?
DORRY. No sir.
ASA. I don't get visitors out here, as a rule, unless someone in th
family has died. It is considered acceptable for me to attend funerals.
DORRY. No one died.
ASA. Not weddings mind you. Only funerals.

(Again it is uncomfortable.)

DORRY. You fixing that chair up?
ASA. Mmh.
DORRY. It looks old.
ASA. It ought to. I found it in the attic, pieces scattered all over th
place. Don't know how old it is, but certainly a lot older than either one o
us. Maybe back 'fore the Civil War. *(Gesturing toward the house.)* Part o
the house goes back that far. Course this ain't the mansion. Yankees burne
that. Don't know why they left this part standing. Raped the women, th
white women. And according to the family history killed your namesake
Shot her in the back as she was running into the swamp seeking refuge.
DORRY. You think that's true?
ASA. Oh, yeah. Too much written about it for it not to be true. Tim
the Yankees got down here they were mad and not interested in showin
mercy. Don't misunderstand me slavery was abhorrent. You believe that
don't you?
DORRY. Yes sir.
ASA. But it was war. There's always Mi Lais when there's war. Yo
know what Mi Lai was?
DORRY. In Viet Nam.
ASA. Mmh. In Viet Nam. Your namesake all them years ago was sho
in the back as she ran screaming into the swamp ... but I have no doubt, i
the Confederacy would of been winning, it'd been the same. There ar
always Mi Lais. *(There is a thermos, large, and he pours himself a drink.)*
You want something to drink?
DORRY. No thank you.
ASA. So what did you come out here for? Did you come out here
because of my eternal soul? Did my sister send you out here because she
wishes for me to be greeted with favor by St. Peter as I come to the Pearly
Gates?
DORRY. Momma doesn't know I'm here.
ASA. Mmh.
DORRY. I thought it best not to tell her.

ASA. So you've made the sojourn on your own?

DORRY. Yes sir.

ASA. You have come to help me understand that I am aberrant. I'm surprised you're not packing the Holy Bible like a revolver ready to fire those words at me that damn my eternal soul.

DORRY. No Bible.

ASA. Then what do you want? You knew your mother wouldn't want you —

DORRY. I don't care what she wants!!!

ASA. *(Seeing that there is something serious, more gentle now.)* What brought you here?

DORRY. *(Softly)* I'm like you?

ASA. You're what?

DORRY. Like you.

ASA. You've been cast out from the family?

DORRY. No.

ASA. Then what are you trying to say?

DORRY. I'm a homosexual.

(A long pause.)

ASA. You are?

DORRY. Yes.

ASA. You're a lesbian?

DORRY. Unhun.

ASA. Oh, my!

DORRY. Yeah.

ASA. What does my sister say about this?

DORRY. She doesn't know.

ASA. I see. *(There is a long pause.)* Are you sure you wouldn't like a drink. *(He is pouring his drink into a cup.)* It's got a little kick to it.

DORRY. Maybe a little.

(He pours her a drink. Maybe it's a thermos with a cup lid that he might not necessarily be drinking from. It is important that the extra cup make sense as far as the story is concerned. He pours it.)

ASA. There you go.

DORRY. *(She sips. She winces.)* It's got a little more than a little kick to it.

ASA. Has it? I'm sorry. I don't notice anymore.

(Another pause.)

DORRY. No one knows. That's why I'm here.

ASA. Ah.
DORRY. I came here because no one knows and ...
ASA. And?
DORRY. And I know you are.
ASA. Homosexual?
DORRY. Yes. You are? Aren't you?
ASA. Undoubtedly.
DORRY. Good.
ASA. *(Smiling)* Good?
DORRY. Yes. I mean ... well ... what I meant to say is good for me that you are ... otherwise you ... I'm just –
ASA. It's all right.
DORRY. That's why I'm here, cause you are. I need to talk to someone who understands ... who can give me some advice.
ASA. Hold that horse.
DORRY. What's wrong? I just need someone to talk to.
ASA. It's the advice part that's the problem.
DORRY. Who else am I supposed to talk to?
ASA. I don't know.
DORRY. You're the only homosexual I know.
ASA. I'm sure that's not true.
DORRY. Yes, it is.
ASA. What about your girlfriends?
DORRY. I don't have any girlfriends.
ASA. I thought you were a lesbian.
DORRY. I am. But I've never had a girlfriend.
ASA. Oh. Never?
DORRY. Never.
ASA. Are you sure you're a lesbian?
DORRY. I'm sure.
ASA. But you've never?
DORRY. No. But I know. You believe me, don't you?
ASA. I don't suppose you'd go making something like that up.
DORRY. So you see why you're the only person I can come to for advice.
ASA. Well let me assure you that the reports of my misery are greatly exaggerated.
DORRY. But you live out here in the swamp.
ASA. That's what I choose. I got a little money, I don't have to be out here. It's my choice.
DORRY. I know, but – the prejudice.
ASA. Prejudice my ass. There are plenty of places I could go where the prejudice is certainly abideable.
DORRY. But there shouldn't be –
ASA. As far as I can see that's just the way of the world. Just let me assure you I'm here totally by choice.

DORRY. I just wish I could believe you.

ASA. *(Getting riled.)* If you're not going to believe me what's the point of coming out here?

DORRY. I thought ...

ASA. You thought what? That there would be some huge reunion scene between yourself and your faggot uncle?

DORRY. I guess maybe.

ASA. God that's ... I think you should go on and get out of here. I got work to do.

DORRY. I didn't mean to make you angry. I just always thought that you must have been so hurt —

ASA. Well, you thought wrong. And that's the first thing you need to learn about being queer. *(DORRY looks as if she's been hit by a stun gun. ASA notices her as she stands there pale.)* What's the matter?

DORRY. Nothing.

ASA. *(Pouring a drink.)* Here drink this. *(She does, he looks at her. Figuring it out.)* Ain't no one ever called you a queer before?

DORRY. No.

ASA. *(Trying to pull her out of her shock.)* Well, unless you plan on staying in the closet all your life, you might as well get used to it. Cause you're going to be called queer and worse.

DORRY. I know.

ASA. Queer, dyke, faggot, muff diver —

DORRY. I know the words. You don't need to name them all.

ASA. That'd take up most of the day. And if the worst thing that happens to you is that you get called queer once in a while, then you're lucky. But being a lezzie is different than being a faggot. It can be chic and fashionable to be a lesbian ... faggots are at best oversensitive men and at worst queers. But that's just my opinion and I don't know anything about being a lesbian. But I was trying to make a point before you got yourself all shocked at being called queer.

DORRY. I'm sorry.

ASA. No need to be.

DORRY. It just stopped everything ... that's not it ... I don't know.

ASA. Sort of like your first kiss — but not good?

DORRY. Like that.

ASA. *(Gentle)* It's a right of passage. The first time someone calls you queer and means it. And first it makes you mad but then you realize it's the truth.

DORRY. Like an explosion — but quiet.

ASA. Mmh. Better not give it too much thought though. If there's anything I'd feel safe saying to you it's don't make anymore out of being queer than what you have to. Not any of it is as important as it might seem.

DORRY. But it's what I am.

ASA. Queer?

DORRY. Well, there's other words I prefer, but yeah.

ASA. That's what you are?

DORRY. You know it is.

ASA. It's not what I am. I'm just a man trying to get through life.

DORRY. Yeah, but you like men.

ASA. Right now, that's a infinitesimal part of my getting through life. And that's all I got to say is just keep it all within perspective.

DORRY. All right.

ASA. You sound disappointed.

DORRY. No.

ASA. I think you are.

DORRY. Least you talked to me.

ASA. Yeah. But ... ?

DORRY. I guess I got a little carried away. In my head. Carried away ...

ASA. I see.

DORRY. It's taken a long time. A long time to come out here. I've planned to do this for some time. Years. Been thinking what it would be like to come and talk to you. But ... I'd be all ready to come ... get everything planned ... figure out a way so that no one would know I was coming ... and then something'd happen. Every time I'd get ready to come something would happen. I'd plan on coming out here to the swamp place ... that's what momma calls it, the old swamp place.

ASA. I know. She told me that it was a fitting place for me to be. Out here with the reptiles and varmints. Fitting place for me to live.

DORRY. She don't mean half what she says.

ASA. She means it.

DORRY. She don't know what she's talking about.

ASA. She knows.

DORRY. What I'm trying to say is that I finally figured out that the reason I was never making it out here ... the reason all those things were happening ... was because I was ... I had a lot of trepidation about coming out here, talking to you.

ASA. Your mother hasn't painted –

DORRY. No, that's not it. I don't know what I was afraid of ... I guess it's cause coming out here ... there'd be things I'd have to say ... and I guess I was trying not to say them ... because if they weren't said then none of it was real ... although I wanted to ... am I making any sense at all?

ASA. Unhun.

DORRY. It wasn't fear.

ASA. It's just that coming here concretized everything.

DORRY. Huh?

ASA. Concretized. Made it solid. Real.

DORRY. Is that a real word?

ASA. I use it. You understand it. It's a word. That's what happened when I called you queer. It just made it all real.

DORRY. I guess what I need to do is decide if I want to tell them.
ASA. Your mom and dad?
DORRY. Unhun.
ASA. About –
DORRY. About being a lesbian.
ASA. You don't bring that horse around here. I'm not having anything
to do with it.
DORRY. I just want to know what you think I –
ASA. I think that's up to you.
DORRY. You told.
ASA. Not exactly. Look, I think there's some things ... you go digging
round out there in the swamp ... you don't know what you won't find.
DORRY. But you did tell.
ASA. Not exactly.
DORRY. Then how do they all know?
ASA. Discovered in flagrante delicto.
DORRY. Oh.
ASA. 'Fraid so.
DORRY. Who?
ASA. Let it go.
DORRY. Momma?
ASA. Mmh.
DORRY. Oh God. And she told everyone.
ASA. Mmh.
DORRY. Damn her.
ASA. She had her reasons.
DORRY. Her religious hypocrisy.
ASA. Don't be –
DORRY. What?
ASA. Rough on her.
DORRY. What? Something else.
ASA. Nothing.
DORRY. What happened?
ASA. I've said all I need to.
DORRY. It's my right to know.
ASA. No.
DORRY. Maybe not my right ... but you're my uncle. She's my
mother. Ever since I can remember I've heard her rage on and on about you
and your immorality ... about the unmentionable acts you engage in. I'd
like to know if she's going to think the same thing about me if she finds out.
ASA. She won't. It's different.
DORRY. How's it so different?
ASA. You're a daughter.
DORRY. You are her brother.
ASA. Just let it go ... don't go digging –

DORRY. I'm going to find out.

ASA. You're liable to exhume things which you'll wish were le buried.

DORRY. Why did momma freak out –

ASA. I suppose she was shocked ... didn't know that men ... men di those sort of things with one another ...

DORRY. I don't believe you.

ASA. Mayhaps she felt moral outrage ... found herself overcome b the spirit of the Almighty and compelled to spew forth the judgment o God.

DORRY. Why was she so angry?

ASA. Because of the person I was with.

DORRY. Who?

ASA. Her intended.

DORRY. Oh.

ASA. So you see. It wouldn't be the same with you.

DORRY. No.

ASA. She had a right to be angry.

(There is a long silence.)

DORRY. How could you ... you know?

ASA. I didn't set out to ... no one thought ... everyone was young Younger than you ... your mother ... I'm not sure why ... it was here ... th little field over there ... the live oak ... after it was all over ... I alway thought it would be struck by lightning ... but it never has been ... it wa there ... and ... what can I say ... she was angry ... who wouldn't be ... yo know it was over 30 years ago ... I might have hoped the fire woul dissipate by now ... but ... she still has that eternal flame of God's rage ... a the time I didn't even know it was important ... that took a while to set in . and in retrospect ... in my musing out here at night when the fog comes i off the swamp and cocoons me ... that's when I can think ... I suppose fron a distance it all seems very Biblical.

DORRY. What?

ASA. Nothing.

DORRY. Biblical?

ASA. The tree ... and your mother's intended ... it was my first ... an she came upon it ... ant then ran back through the fields towards the house ... the house where everyone was ... I think it was a birthday celebration fo one of the old ones ... something like that ... back then they used to come t the old place ... here to the swamp ... and she ran back screaming ... I trie to stop her. We both tried to stop her ... but she was running and screamin toward the house and they ran out of the house ... thinking there must be rogue gator or something on the loose ... maybe a wild boar'd come in ou of the swamp ... and we're running after her half dressed ... and she'

running as if a swarm of bees have settled in her hair ... and then ... there
was quiet ... and everything was changed forever ... and God turned his
back on me and took his angels away. Your mother's right to be angry ...
but if you get a chance let her know that there has been some small amount
of punishment.
    DORRY. I'm sorry.
    ASA. So am I.
    DORRY. Yes.
    ASA. I suspect we all are.
    DORRY. I didn't know mother was engaged to anyone but dad. She
always said he was her first love.
    ASA. He was.
    DORRY. Oh.

(After a long pause.)

    ASA. I told you this is –
    DORRY. I know. And if I go digging ... I see that ... I understand why
mother doesn't want you around.
    ASA. Yes.
    DORRY. I never had ...
    ASA. No. Of course not.
    DORRY. Never would I have thought –

(Long pause.)

    ASA. Are you all right?
    DORRY. I don't know. A little overwhelmed.
    ASA. It would be best if you not say anything to them, there's
no need –
    DORRY. No. I won't. Would never.
    ASA. Good.
    DORRY. My father?
    ASA. Mmh.
    DORRY. Was my father ...
    ASA. He was young. Must have been 18 at the oldest. It was one of
those things – it ended up with a lot of meaning ... but it didn't initially
mean anything.
    DORRY. I think it did. You –
    ASA. Not to him.
    DORRY. Oh.
    ASA. Just ... you know boys ... Young men.
    DORRY. Ah.
    ASA. Raging hormones ... the smell of the swamp – a breeze from the
gulf, a feel of electricity in the air. But there was no meaning. And no
control.

DORRY. She must have loved him a great deal to forgive him.
ASA. I wouldn't –
DORRY. To take him as her husband despite –
ASA. Yes.
DORRY. He doesn't speak poorly of you.
ASA. Mmh.
DORRY. Sometimes he tells her to let it go ... to just forget –
ASA. You don't need to tell me this –
DORRY. Of course I thought he meant your lifestyle ... but now I see ...
ASA. Don't think –
DORRY. It always seemed to make him sad ...
ASA. It made us all sad ...
DORRY. Did he have feelings for –
ASA. No, I told you it was just ... Nothing ... Nothing to him ... And if she had not seen ... it would have been nothing to anyone.
DORRY. It was a rite of passage.
ASA. Mmh.
DORRY. Your first. That's what you said. It would still have been that.

(He is having another drink. This is not the first, second, or third.)

ASA. Oh yes that. Well, that doesn't relate to them ... that's just ... just ... my ... my ... that's mine.
DORRY. You're all right?
ASA. Of course. It's you that I'm worried about.
DORRY. No. I'm ...
ASA. Nothing new to me ... it's what I live with.
DORRY. I suppose I should –
ASA. Yes. I need to see if I can get this all back together again. *(Meaning the piece of furniture he's working on.)* And you're distracting me.
DORRY. You sure you got all the pieces?
ASA. Oh, they're here all right. Just got to get them all in the right place. Don't be disappointed ... I suspect you're one of those people who feels a great amount of sympathy for poor Asa who lives out there in the swamp ...
DORRY. Empathy ...
ASA. And it seems as if everyone tries to somehow make it about the prejudices and the bigotry of others ... their ignorance and what has been done to me because of it ... concoct a very sad story ... where there is good and bad clearly defined ... I suspect you did a little of that ... thought that there'd be this tremendous bond between the two of us ... because of the queer thing ... but it's all wrong. My story doesn't have a lot to do with that ... no, the sadness of my life has at its heart a significant betrayal.

DORRY. Yes. It seems that way. *(He has another drink.)* I suppose I should be on my way.

ASA. Mmh.

DORRY. I'm glad I came. I understand momma more ...

ASA. Glad I can be of help.

DORRY. I'll come back to see you.

ASA. No need.

DORRY. No. But I will.

ASA. Mmh.

DORRY. I will.

ASA. Sometimes I think that's what life is.

DORRY. Mmh.

ASA. All life is.

DORRY. *(Not really wanting to talk further.)* Is what?

ASA. A series of betrayals.

DORRY. That doesn't give a person much to look forward to.

ASA. A series of betrayals. Surviving a series of betrayals until finally the body betrays the spirit and then you have the last of the betrayals. That's what your mother doesn't know ... she just stayed here ... she didn't go out ... she doesn't understand that she doesn't hold the copyright on betrayals.

DORRY. I think what happened would certainly make her a member of the club ... considering the circumstances ... and all ... it would seem that she understands ...

ASA. She doesn't understand anymore than what anyone can understand when you're young and ... and neither can you ... yes I betrayed her. And there was a time when I begged her to forgive me ... did you know that? I don't suppose so. And I don't suppose she owes telling anyone any of it. But she said it was something that she couldn't forgive ... and then the family they agreed with her. And they sent me away ... I went up north ... up around Tupelo ... where Elvis was born ... and stayed with cousins ... who didn't know what had happened ... the family wouldn't ever really let me be a part of it again ... except for my dad ... who left me these forty acres ... much to everyone else's chagrin, I might add ... but them doing that ... was understandable just like your mother ... what she did was understandable ... but what was not understandable was that all of a sudden my Master ... had said depart from me ... it was something I didn't know ... that the Lord God Almighty ... was not mine ... had nothing to do with me ... that I was an abomination to him ... and I had been told that he loved all the children of the world ... and now I was betrayed ... and when I grew up and left ... and ... I was with people who considered God a crutch for the weak ... but what they didn't understand is I needed that crutch ... I was weak and I needed ... I needed my angels ... but if I believed what so many said I was part of a godless lot ... and that's something ... that's a betrayal too ... when your God becomes your Judas. That's why I came back ...

Don't think I was miserable ... I've lived all over this country ... and I've had one night stands ... more than I can count ... and some meaningful relationships too ... meaningful encounters can come in the strangest of disguises ... but I came back because ... because ... I wanted to see if the angels were still here.

DORRY. The angels?

ASA. In antebetrayal times ... by that I mean ante like in antebellum ... in those times there were angels out here ... I need them ... Your momma and I, we used to go out where the swamp begins ... where the alligators lie in wait ... where the cypress hang heavy with Spanish moss and the fog drips like tears from the eyes of all the once lovely people who have lost the battle to age and weep for beauty past. Your momma and I we'd come out here, when twilight was stealing across the lea and we'd look up at the moss and, and watch for angels ... and we'd see them sometimes ... their wings winnowing the air. Your momma, she'd take me when I was just a little thing ... she's the one that taught me how to see them ... we'd come down and see the moss move as the angels' wings ... and then all that happened ... and I never saw them ... never saw the angels ... after your momma and I would go down here ... mind you I was only six or seven at first ... but I used to imagine the angels following us back up here and when I'd go to sleep at night I could feel them wrap their wings around me keeping me safe ... everyone was so poor back then ... your momma and the angels were the only comfort I had ... and things were never the same since ... and when it all started going wrong ... and haywire out there ... I came back here looking for the angels.

DORRY. Did you find them?

ASA. I'm not sure ... sometimes when twilight is stealing I think I might ... but I'm not a little boy with his older sister now ... it's not so easy now ... it's not so easy to see them ... to believe ... but I desperately want them to be there.

DORRY. Lord knows.

ASA. I got an idea.

DORRY. *(Cannot help but ask.)* You know I never saw you at anything but funerals ... no one talks much about you ... 'cept of course ... you know.

ASA. Mmh.

DORRY. How much older is momma than you?

ASA. Don't.

DORRY. You were talking about how momma was older and she taught you about the angels, how much older is she than you?

ASA. What does it –

DORRY. I can look it up.

ASA. Do you really want to?

DORRY. Just answer me.

ASA. Five years. Almost to the day ... March babies. Born under the sign of Pisces.

DORRY. Momma got married when she was 18?

ASA. That's right.

DORRY. So the day she found you and my father out there under the ve oak ... she was seventeen. Right?

ASA. Seventeen – just turned eighteen I believe.

DORRY. And daddy he would have been –

ASA. Eighteen. Leave it.

DORRY. And you?

ASA. Thirteen. *(She reacts.)* Don't even think those thoughts. Times vere different. Don't make it ugly. Don't make it vulgar. Leave it be.

DORRY. You were thirteen.

ASA. Leave me my right of passage with some dignity, please.

DORRY. How could they send you away, blame you?

ASA. Different time ... don't try to judge ... that ... it never works to do hat ... we were poor. Just the swamp place ... and you were on the way ... veryone did what they thought was best.

DORRY. But ...

ASA. Leave it ... if you want to hang around with me ... and walk down o the edge of the swamp and look for angels ... that I owe you ... it's what our momma did for me ... and after that day I don't imagine she's seen hem since ... never took you down to see them ... I'd like to do that ... it's uite wonderful when you see them winnowing ... but I'm not interested in alking about the other – sad people sit around and talk about betrayals.

DORRY. All right.

ASA. *(Almost timid.)* Won't be long it'll be twilight. You want to wait round and go down to the place where the Yankees shot your great, great, reat, great in the back ... when I was a child that was the spot where we nost frequently spied the angels. If you've got the time that is.

DORRY. I got the time.

END OF PLAY

COSTUME PLOT

ASA:
Work clothes, not very well kept.

DORRY:
Feminine colors, dress or skirt preferred.

PROPERTY PLOT

Old piece of furniture, such as chair or bench, in sections
Thermos with cup-type lid

GROUND PLAN

A swamp. A bare stage is all that is necessary.